INTER FERENCE & Other Stories

n e w

RIVERS PRESS MSUM

American Fiction Series

INTER
FERENCE
& Other Stories

Richard Hoffman

© 2009 by Richard Hoffman
First Edition
Library of Congress Control Number: 2008934509
ISBN: 978-0-89823-247-9
American Fiction Series
Cover design by Megan McCleary
Author photograph by Mike Lew

The publication of *Interference and Other Stories* is made possible by the generous support of the McKnight Foundation and other contributors to New Rivers Press.

For academic permission please contact Frederick T. Courtright at 570-839-7477 or permdude@eclipse.net. For all other permissions, contact The Copyright Clearance Center at 978-750-8400 or info@copyright.com.

New Rivers Press is a nonprofit literary press associated with Minnesota State University Moorhead.

Wayne Gudmundson, Director
Alan Davis, Senior Editor
Donna Carlson, Managing Editor
Allen Sheets, Art Director
Thom Tammaro, Poetry Editor
Kevin Carollo, MVP Poetry Coordinator
Liz Severn, MVP Fiction Coordinator
Frances Zimmerman, Business Manager
    Publishing Interns: Samantha Jones, Andrew Olson, Mary Huyck Mulka
    Interference Book Team: Michael Beeman, Kayla Lundgren,
        Tarver Mathison, Alyssa Schafer
    Editorial Interns: Michael Beeman, Nathan Logan, Kayla Lundgren,
        Tarver Mathison, Mary Huyck Mulka, Amber Olds, Jessica Riepe,
        Alyssa Schafer, Andrea Vasquez
    Design Interns: Alex Ehlen, Andrew Kerr, Erin Malkowski, Megan McCleary,
        Lindsay Stokes

Printed in the United States of America.

New Rivers Press
c/o MSUMoorhead
1104 7th Avenue South
Moorhead, MN 56563
www.newriverspress.com

for Kathi, as always

CONTENTS

NOTHING TO LOOK AT HERE

The bikes buzzed past trooper Larry Powell in the unmarked car, three of them, then another two, and then after a moment one more, all of them going ninety, maybe more, weaving in and out of the three lanes of interstate traffic, so he hit the blue light and siren and pursued. Ahead, he saw several drivers swerve as they became aware of the sudden noise and color of the bikes whizzing past them — a dangerous set of circumstances, goddamn it, somebody could get killed. He was on the straggler quickly, moving right up behind him, holding steady, until the green and yellow crotch rocket, a Kawasaki, a "rice-burner," they would have called it at the barracks, slowed and pulled over just beyond a fenced overpass festooned with American flags and a sign: "Welcome Home Pfc. Bruce McHale". Powell radioed his whereabouts and action as he rolled to a stop on the shoulder about ten yards beyond the bike.

He put on his trooper's hat and walked back to the rider. "Dismount, please." No response. "Get off the bike, sir. Now." The rider dismounted. "And remove your helmet, sir."

The rider was a young man, maybe eighteen, maybe younger. Sir. Ha. He held the bright enameled shell of the helmet under his arm. Dark eyes. Eurasian features.

"License and registration."

"Officer, can I just say — "

Powell raised his hand so quickly the young man flinched. "Don't," Powell said. "Let's have it. Right now." His hand moved from the stop to the give-me position; he even snapped his fingers. "Remain here. You understand? You seem to have a little trouble following simple directions."

Powell returned to the car, ran the computer check. Holder, Lee. Date of birth, 9/18/87. Clean. The bike was, of course, a rental.

It took another moment before the date registered: Holder had been born on the same day as Powell's late son, Franklin, though he was three years younger than Franklin would now have been. Powell watched the young man in the rearview mirror and thought his posture arrogant, arms crossed over his chest as if to say to passing drivers that it's worth the price of a stupid ticket once in a while to have some fun. Not like the rest of you losers. The young man ran the toe of his sneaker back and forth in a little half-moon in the ground, and Powell took this to mean he was disinterested and impatient to get this over with and be on his way.

Well, let him wait then, Powell thought, let him stand there shifting his weight back and forth. This is what his girlfriend Didi would call a teachable moment. A school psychologist, she would have weighed in here on the value of consequences, and on the necessity of spelling out the connection between action and consequence. No argument from Powell. When Franklin hit the bridge abutment and broke his neck, he'd been going eighty, and the autopsy showed a blood alcohol level of 0.25, making it questionable whether or not Franklin had even been conscious when he lost control of the car. Even so, just days after his burial, his friends had held a night-time party on his grave, leaving behind a copy of the yearbook, a dozen beer cans, and an empty quart of Jim Beam. Somebody'd puked, too. Some memorial. It seemed fair to say that they had trouble connecting actions to consequences. The difference between him and Didi — aside from the aggravating fact that she didn't think they should be married — was that she was ready with explanations having to do with the slow maturation of the pre-frontal lobe, where the kind of cognition that weighs actions and consequences occurs; for Powell, it was just needless stupidity and it made him angry. The other difference, of course, was that Franklin was not her son.

Franklin's mother, Liz, who was raised and still had family in Minnesota, moved there even before the divorce was final. Whenever he thought about it, Powell chose to keep it simple: the marriage did not survive the death of their only child. Period. It was true that she'd said he was too hard on their son and blamed him for the boy's defiant wildness, which she saw as the cause of the accident; and it was also true that Powell had never managed to talk himself out of his conviction that Liz was no good at setting limits and that if she couldn't handle the boy's defiance as he got older, then she should not have interposed herself between him, the stronger disciplinarian, and their son. But those mutual recriminations were much too painful to revisit, and — even more painfully — irrelevant now.

"So why don't you want to get married, Miss Texas? Don't people get married down there where you grew up?"

"I already told you. I don't see why."

"Because it's a commitment."

"Larry, I'm not going anywhere. What is with this marriage thing? Right now I think it's great having a lover. And you're a great lover."

"Oh throw me a bone, why don't you?" Powell smirked, but he was pleased to hear she thought so. "I thought women were supposed to want to be married. "

"Darlin', sometimes you are one big beefcake bimbo, you know that? Let me tell you something. There are only two things you need to remember about women. The first is that we're just like you. And the second is that we're different creatures entirely because we're always having to contend with what you men imagine us to be."

"Is that supposed to clarify things?"

She raised herself onto one elbow and pinched lightly at his left nipple. She often played around with his nipples, something no woman had ever done before. He didn't find it unpleasant, but it didn't do much for him either. "Darlin', marriage is just the next stop on the bus you're on. But you know what? It's a tour bus. It goes in a circle. So, no thanks. I want you in my life, Larry. I do. But marriage? No thanks."

Powell made a face at her that he hoped was an equal mix of disappointment and reproach, a look that would say he was hurt but that she'd blown it, that it was her loss, and brushed her hand away from his chest.

His helmet under his arm, the young man was approaching the car now, no doubt to ask if he could have his ticket and be on his way. Powell watched him in the rearview mirror for a moment and gathered himself for the display of power and authority called for in this situation. It was straight out of academy procedures and it always worked. He stepped from the car, wheeled, and pointing at arm's length as he strode toward the youth, he yelled, "You will return to your vehicle, sir, and remain there!" The young man, stunned, stumbled and almost fell as he double-timed it back to the bike.

Powell returned to the car but this time left the door open and one jackbooted leg outside for emphasis. The few times he'd had to use this maneuver before, he'd enjoyed it: the rush of adrenaline (after all, an individual approaching the car from behind could be dangerous), the outsized and theatrical quality of it, the legally sanctioned bullying it involved. This time he noted that the young man was taller than he and though still lanky, he had begun to fill out; that, and the startled fear on the young man's face at Powell's sudden ferocity, had instead disturbed him and he felt a momentary regret at the way the whole interaction was unfolding.

It had been the third time Powell spent the night at her place that Didi told him that she had known Franklin. They were lying in her bed, awake in the dark, the headlights of passing cars making the bright ghost of the window slide across the ceiling and down the wall.

"I didn't want to tell you right away. Because."

"Because?" But what Powell was thinking was that she was a school shrink and she had known Franklin and here she was dating him so he couldn't have been the dad from hell who drove his kid right over the edge, right?

"Well, lots of reasons, I guess. I didn't want you to think I was feeling sorry for you. Of course I was. Feeling sorry for you. But not just that."

"What, then?"

"Oh, Darlin', I don't know! I was drawn to you. Not everything can be explained."

"Ah! I like that. 'Not everything can be explained.' May I quote you?"

"What is with you, tonight?"

"I don't know." Powell had now heard two things that made him feel better than he had in a while. He thought he should probably quit while he was ahead. "Go on," he said.

"I don't know, I said. I liked your dignity. Your resilience."

"And all along I was thinking you just wanted to get in my pants."

"We call that projecting, Darlin'."

"I just called it hoping."

She slapped at him affectionately.

"So did he ever, you know, talk to you? Franklin?"

"I know who you mean."

"Well?"

"This isn't right, Larry. I can't."

"You brought it up."

"I'm sorry. I wish I hadn't. It was inappropriate."

"Inappropriate. Now there's a shrinky-dink word for you."

"All I said was that I knew him."

"Yes, but he talked to you. You as much as said so."

"I did not."

"Well you didn't deny it. You could have said no. That you didn't know him like that. You could have just said he was in your teen health class or something."

"Let me tell you something, Larry." She put her hand on his face, turned it toward her. "I will never lie to you. I promise you that."

He tried to turn his head away; she was surprisingly strong.

"If I ever think there is anything your boy told me that you need to know, I will tell you. Now, good night." She kissed him and rolled away.

Powell watched the window's bright white negatives patrol the wall and ceiling until he fell asleep.

The day of the accident he'd been working the turnpike at one of his favorite spots. He parked on the shoulder and aimed the doppler gun at a rise that kept him invisible. As cars gained the rise, the gun read the highest speed so the first one to come into view was his mark. He'd been writing tickets all afternoon. He received the news from dispatch. "How bad?"

"I'd get there right away. Larry, I'm sorry."

So he knew immediately. And putting that information in a safe place inside himself, he turned on the lights and siren and headed as instructed for the North River Family Clinic, the nearest healthcare facility to the accident. Next thing he knew he was looking at a poster of Big Bird, his long orange legs with some kind of red quoits around them he had never noticed before, and on the wall behind him on his left Bert with his tufted head shaped like an egg right next to walnut-headed Ernie, so that he looked right away at the wall over to his right as if it were a complete this series problem — wait! Who did he expect to see there? Grover? Cookie Monster? Elmo? The Count? Anything, ask any question, look anywhere, anywhere but at the body of his son there on the butcher's paper of the examining table against the wall in front of him.

And that had been the astonishing thing to him, a fact so wondrous and filled with hope he felt a stab of joy: this isn't my son, this can't be my son, why, this is the body of a grown man!

Someone asked him if he wanted a chair, which he refused with a gesture as he leaned over the body and placed one hand on each shoulder. The smell of alcohol was overpowering. There was no blood. He wanted to sit the boy up, to gather him in, but all he could do was stare and shake his head from side to side. Then he patted the boy's shoulder quickly five times with his hand as if consoling him: Don't worry about it; there's always next time. Then he straightened, about-faced, and strode from the room.

Liz had been notified and was waiting at home for him. Her friend, Donna, was there, along with their minister, Tom Emery, and Captain Whalen, his boss. As he embraced Liz he already knew from the way he held her and the way she held herself back from him that the marriage would not survive. He always wanted to ask her afterwards if she had already known, too.

And this young man, Lee Holder — what was to be done with him and his whole pack of maniacs with their undeveloped pre-fucking-frontal common sense? He looked up at the rearview mirror and finally set about writing the summons. Speeding, yes. Driving to endanger, yes. Reckless driving, yes. DUI, no — no indication of alcohol at all. But he didn't check any of the boxes; instead he took the clipboard with him and walked back to where the youth stood by the bike, looking down now.

"Mr. Holder."

"Yes, sir."

And then they both heard them, the steadily gaining hum of the others as they approached on the other side of the Interstate, returning, tamed now, just below the speed limit, to look for him. Clearly they had spotted him because they got off at the ramp and massed on the overpass, straddling their bikes and watching from behind the cyclone fence.

"Your friends came looking for you."

Just the slightest nod from the young man.

"Mr. Holder, I am authorized by the commonwealth to cite you for speeding, for driving to endanger, and for reckless driving. All three are moving violations. The first requires payment of a fine of one hundred dollars plus ten dollars for each mile beyond the speed limit. I have entered your speed here at ninety miles per hour. Do you know what the speed limit is on the interstate?"

"Fifty-five."

"That is correct. The remaining two violations require appearance before a magistrate of the court who may demand surrender of your license to operate a motor vehicle, or mandatory attendance at driver's school, or both." Powell was watching the young man's face intently as he said this, although what he was looking for he could not have said. He looked up at the colorful band of onlookers for a moment, then he checked only the speeding box on the citation and handed it to the young man.

A semi hurtled past, its wind shear almost tearing the ticket from Holder's hand. They both raised their hands to their faces as the wave of gritty air broke over them.

"In the future, please exercise more caution, Mr. Holder. Good day now." He turned to go back to the car.

"Officer?"

"Yes?"

"Can I say something? I mean, may I?"

Powell turned back to face him, and noted again the bright gallery assembled on the overpass.

"We were being stupid. Sorry."

Powell kept a stern look on his face, but he was too near the edge of his grief now to even chance meeting the young man's eyes. He touched two fingers to the wide brim of his trooper's hat and strode back to the car double-time, as if he had somewhere to go and was late.

"But why not? I still don't get it."

They were at Powell's, in his bed, which he preferred to Didi's because it was a king. Because every three months he worked the eleven-to-seven shift, he'd bought room-darkening shades for all the windows, and usually he slept well here, another reason he preferred his place to Didi's.

"Because Darlin', I don't want to be a piece of furniture, okay? Let's see. I need a sofa, some chairs, a table, and oh, yeah, a wife. Hmmmm. This one looks pretty good. How soon can I have it delivered?"

"What?"

"Look, a little perspective wouldn't kill you, you know. Studies have been done, and —"

"Oh! Studies! Studies have been done!"

"Yes, and you know what they found? That cops have the highest rates of divorce of any profession, but hold on, Darlin', here's the good part — they also have the highest rate of remarriage. It's like ninety percent. Ninety percent!" She got out of bed. "I'd rather be the woman in your heart, Larry, okay? Not the new marriage that proves to the guys at the barracks, and to your ex, and to yourself that you're fine." His hat was there on the chair next to the phone on the nightstand — round and brown and chin-strapped and dented just so — and she put it on and slipped into a loud, deep, officer-at-the-accident voice: "It's okay folks. Everything's fine here, folks. Nothing to look at here. Keep it moving." Naked except for the hat, she gesticulated at imaginary rubberneckers, her breasts bobbing and swaying with the movements of her arms. "Nothing to look at here. Keep it moving, folks. Nothing to look at here."

Powell felt his face flush, blood and anger and shame all coming to the surface. He whipped the covers off and stood and glared at her across the bed. How dare she? He had imagined the scene a hundred times before he managed to lay it to rest: the cruisers, the lights, Tom Whalen and troopers Stern and Korofsky on the scene,

Franklin's Nissan crumpled in the weeds, his boy, unbloodied, who would get no older. And one of them, probably Korofsky, waving the traffic on by. He moved his mouth but nothing came out.

"Oh my god, Larry. That's not what I meant. I didn't think. Oh my god, I'm sorry. I'm such an idiot! I'm sorry!"

"Out," he managed. He pointed to the door. "Get dressed and get out." He turned and sat on the bed with his back to her, struggling with himself.

"Larry. Darlin'. I'm so sorry."

He could hear her approaching around the bed and he stood and wheeled and pointed, something like the maneuver he'd used with the Holder kid. "Go!" he said, "Now!"

He watched her shrink and back up two steps before he turned away. He sat back on the bed and listened to her gather up her things and dress in the other room. Even before he heard the front door close, he'd changed his mind, but he couldn't call out to her.

Though he already knew he would not sleep, he turned out the light. But tonight the dark was not friendly, and he lay in a box of black, a weight on his chest and bedlam in his head. He was not so much thinking as suffering thought: it came out of the opaque emptiness from all directions and converged on him. Memories and fears and anger and recriminations. Faces and voices. Liz, Franklin, Didi. No single thought that he might fix and consider. Consciousness itself a black cascade.

All the alternatives to simply lying there letting the torment continue were available — he could put on the light and read; go into the other room and look for a late night movie on TV; he could pour himself a bourbon, just two fingers; he could dress and go out for a walk; he could get in the shower and let the hot water hit the back of his neck and shoulders while he leaned forward, palms on the tile wall — but he refused them, because he trusted some sense he had that he was moving forward. It was like driving at night through a blizzard of regrets and bad faith and lies he'd been told or had told himself. There was nothing to do but try to stay on the road. Later, looking back on this night, he would think that it was a lot like dreaming — the whole process going on without any direction from him, as if his mind were deliberating without him.

Well into the night, he realized he'd been crying, the tears running down across his temples and into his ears, and after that he slept.

Usually, upon waking, he needed two strong cups of Maxwell House before he would attempt anything like conversation, but as soon as he opened his eyes he knew what he needed to do.

Just as her answering machine picked up, Didi answered.

"Hello?"

"Hi. It's Larry." *Hello. You have reached the home of Didi Magruder...*

"Oh for godsakes, this damn thing. Wait. Let me turn it off. How do you turn the damn thing off?" *I can't answer your call right now, but if you'll please leave a message...* "I'm not sure how to do it without cutting you off. You want me to call you back? It'll be done in a minute." *... after the long beep, including your number, even if you think I already have it, I'll return your call just as soon as I can. Thank you.* "Larry? Larry, I am so sorry for what I said. I had no right. I was up all night just sick with shame. I never meant to hurt you, Darlin'. I am such an idiot sometimes. I had no right to get sarcastic."

Powell cut in. "Didi, stop. Stop. I was the one. I was way out of line."

BEEEEEP.

"So you forgive me for being so insensitive?"

"Done. I guess you hit a nerve."

"Larry, I want to tell you something. But now I'm a little afraid I'll say the wrong thing. Listen, I want to tell you something Franklin said to me one time, when he'd come to see me."

Powell moved the hat from the chair next to the bed and sat down. He wasn't sure he trusted her now. Did he want to hear this?

"You said you didn't want to talk about that. And you know what? I can respect that."

"Larry, listen. Oh, what is it with this connection. You sound so far away. Listen. I'd asked about his parents. I didn't know you yet. And he told me he loved the both of you. And when I asked about his dad — and this is what I believe you need to hear now, Darlin', or I wouldn't tell it — he told me that he was not afraid of you. And I believed him, not like with some of the other boys, pumping themselves up so you know the truth is just the opposite; no, I believed him."

"Didi, you don't have to say this stuff. It's okay. Thanks, but it's okay."

"Now see here, Darlin', I'm not finished yet. He said to me, 'My dad gets really mad at me sometimes' — as I recall he said pissed off and then apologized and changed it to mad — 'but one thing I know for sure; no matter what I do wrong, no matter what kind of stupid stuff I pull, he'll always forgive me.' That's what he said, and I know he was telling me the truth the way he saw it, at least at the time."

There was a short beep after which the phone connection was sharper.

"Oh for godsakes, this stupid thing was on the whole time. Are you still there, Darlin'?"

Powell felt like he'd swallowed an ice cube that was melting, painfully, in his chest, and he could barely breathe.

"Larry? Darlin'?"

"Yeah," he said. "Yeah, I'm here."

GUY GOES INTO A BAR

"What'll it be?" asks the bartender.

Guy looks over the bartender's shoulder in the mirror and sees the clock behind him ticking backwards. He scans the bottles. "I'll have the two broken marriages, three fucked-up kids, esophageal bleeding, bankruptcy, white railroad scar from knee to groin from the car crash, the disbarment, three long nights in jail and several hundred hangovers."

"Right-o," says the bartender.

Twenty years later, Guy stands up and stumbles out the door. "No joke," he says when anyone asks him. "I feel like Rip Van Fucking Winkle."

GENTLEMEN

Walter Crosby glanced at the clock above the row of fan belts—five after ten—and shook his head. He was already behind in his work thanks mostly to some goofball kid who was trying to talk him into buying one of those machines that charge people for air.

"I don't sell air," he told the kid while Mrs. Hanley's seventeen-year-old Ford levitated like the miracle it was. He paused, caught the kid's eye, and winked.

"I suck wind sometimes," he grinned, "but I don't sell air." He popped off the right front hubcap, reached for the compressor gun, and squeezed the trigger. *Brrrppt.*

"But you're in business," the kid stammered, "you're in business to make money. To make money. Right?"

Brrrppt. He palmed the lug nut. *Brrrppt.* Another Reagan baby. A suit off the rack, a binder of information, a rap his boss had made him memorize.

"Look, kid, you're wasting time." He dropped the lug nuts in the hubcap. "You're on commission, right? There's nothing here."

The phone rang. "Walter? Walter, it's Donny, Donny D. Your sponsee?"

"Donny, listen. You can just say it's Donny. I only know one Donny." Jesus, was that really even a word, outside AA? Sponsee? But Donny was easy to help; he always needed the same advice.

You can only say slow down so many ways. Be patient. Chill out. Easy Does It. Donny was racing from this to that problem—his bad teeth, his bad marriage, his bad job. One day he might have to haul off and say, "Look, Donny. You destroyed your teeth, your marriage, and your career with booze; now fix what you can and quit your bellyaching." Some sponsors would have done that already, but he sensed that Donny would come to that on his own, that in fact all his worrying was a kind of defense against that insight, and that it was better for him to be a little further along, a little further from his last drink, before he had to feel that particular gut punch.

So Donny was a good fifteen minutes. Then, as soon as he hung up, a cop came by to take a statement about a hit-and-run he'd witnessed two weeks earlier. That was nearly half an hour. When he went back into the bay, the kid was still standing there, sweating in his suit coat. "Just take a minute to look at these figures," he said. He held out a page encased in plastic.

Walter pulled the right front tire, bounced it, and rolled it at the young man who dropped the page, jumped back, threw out his hands and caught it.

"Just roll that over there against the wall."

The kid propped up the tire and turned, holding his blackened hands away from himself.

"Aw, I'm sorry. Don't want to get that suit dirty. Restroom's round the side. Pay in advance, though. Water's damned expensive these days. Mitts black as those?—about a buck a piece I'd say." *Brrrpt.* He was working on the left front tire now. "But hey, tell me something. When you were a little guy, what did you want to be? An air salesman? Tell me. I'd like to know. I really would."

"Screw you, Pops."

"Now that's the spirit! Tell you what. For you? For you the water's free. In fact, I need a man out front for the full-serve pumps and to run the register. You give it some thought while you're washing up. Twelve bucks an hour, no overtime. Best I can do."

When he had lowered Mrs. Hanley's Ford and parked it out front, he called to let her know it was ready. He decided to clean up before replacing the windshield on his daughter Nancy's VW Bug. His son-in-law, Cal, had brought it by that morning. One of the old Beetles, the classic, the windshield was a simple, flat panel held in place with a rubber gasket. The whole job wouldn't take more than an hour. He dipped three fingers in the tub of hand cleaner.

"Leave it to me to park it right under a foul ball," Cal had said. He detailed the flight of the ball off the bat, the few fans in the bleachers on the first base side ducking and covering their heads with their arms, the crunching sound the ball made hitting the VW's windshield.

"Jesus, I was pitching! You can imagine the ragging I took from both benches. Everybody knew whose car it was."

Walter had never learned how to talk to Cal, never knew what to say to him. Some of it, he was sure, had to do with the bizarre and ill-defined categories of son-in-law and father-in-law. Back when he and Emily were married, he never knew what to say to her father, either. Once, while they were visiting her parents' small farm, his mother-in-law, Maureen, had asked him to call her husband in to dinner. He had stepped out on the back porch and could see the man not far off, maybe thirty-five or forty yards away, in front of the barn, with his back to him. Walter had actually raised his hand to the side of his mouth to yell before he realized he didn't even know what to call him. "Jim" was too informal. "Mr. McNulty" too impersonal. "Dad" was out of the question. So he walked there, tapped the man on the shoulder, jerked his head toward the house and said, "Time for dinner."

But Cal seemed like a big kid to him, twenty-seven and still playing baseball in the summer, basketball the rest of the year for one team or another. Four jobs in as many years: driving a cab, a truck, renting office furniture, and now selling ad space for a magazine. As he worked the citrus paste between his fingers, he thought again of the kid who'd come to sell him on turning air to money—what the hell did he know about anything? What the hell does anybody know at that age? Air. Space. Walter shook his head. What a world when this is all the use we can think of for young men.

But Walter felt he was in no position to judge. "Good with his hands," that was him. It was a nice way to say stupid. Why argue? If stupid is drinking yourself out of work, out of love, out of everything that ever mattered to you, then, well, he was good with his hands. He looked at them as he wiped them on a brown paper towel. Blackened and cracked, his knuckles were so scarred they would never tear again. Scar's as good as callous when it comes to that, he thought.

The Mobil station was his refuge. When he'd bought it, three years into his sobriety, two years after the divorce, it was as if he'd withdrawn from the world, the repair bay an anchorite's cave where he spent his days with gears, wires, hoses, pistons, rings, pipes, belts, fuses. What people there were he could manage; their relation was clear. They brought their cars and their complaints: It won't go. It won't stop. It acts up. There were few occasions for rage. Everything was simple. Everything either turns the wheels or stops the wheels or steers the wheels. Never that awful unreason and terror he used to feel with people, a panic that found expression in putting his fist through plasterboard, through wooden doors, through glass. No further cause then for the sickening remorse he still felt sometimes, even twenty-five years later, for his violence, especially in his own home, as a husband, toward Emily. That was a hole you couldn't cover with a picture or a poster. He looked again at his hands and shook his head. Had he really once told Emily she was full of shit because she said he'd broken her jaw when in fact he'd dislocated it? That's how he had been quoted in a letter from her lawyer. He was supposed to have said it on their way home from the ER. Even with no clear memory of the event, he knew it was true.

The young salesman came out of the men's room and walked past the bay to his car. Walter shouted in his direction. "So I guess you're not interested then?"

The kid opened the car door, stared over the roof for a moment, and flipped Walter the bird.

Walter let it ride. He gathered up what he would need to install the new windshield: a length of 14-gauge insulated multistrand wire, a can of silicone spray, a utility knife, large screwdriver, towels, rags, and the new windshield and gasket assembly.

So long as his hands were busy. For more than two decades, so long as his hands were busy, he remained a man who had failed, not a failure. So long as his hands were busy, he was the man who had labored to transform himself, to grieve and go forward, to start again.

When he'd moved out—been thrown out, really—he hadn't had a drink in six months, but his rages, no longer tied to the daily rhythms of his drinking, were less predictable, so worse. He had taken nothing with him to the new apartment: three small rooms, white walls, a mattress on the floor. He tried to empty his life of everything inessential; he would bring things into his life, into his apartment, one at a time, nothing and no one uncertain or unimportant. He took a job at Jiffy Lube, went to AA meetings, and prayed. His sponsor had told him not to worry who or what he was praying to. "Just get down on your knees and ask for help. Leave the theology to the theologians," he'd advised.

He bought a shallow box of sand, a "Zen Garden" the packaging called it, replete with a tiny rake and a book of views of full-sized monastery gardens. He stirred the sand this way and that, stared at the patterns, prayed to the trinity of sand and space and rake. "Gentle me," he said to the white walls, "Please gentle me."

The first time he'd brought Nancy to sleep at the apartment, when she was five, she hadn't even made it to the room he'd fixed up for her before she saw the Zen Garden, the only object in the living room, and ran to it, squealing, "Daddy! You have a kitty!"

There was something so deep and joyous and relieved in his laughter then that the five year old, even in her puzzlement, laughed too, and Walter scooped her up, still laughing, and asked, "Shall we go and buy ourselves a kitty?" And there and then they did.

That evening something else began. Walter never knew how to describe it, since it wasn't, strictly speaking, an event. A shift? A change? An understanding? It began when he was reading Nancy a book that Emily had packed for her. Nancy was next to him on the mattress he'd made up for her, and he felt her staring at the side of his face. When he turned, he was sure he saw his mother gazing from her eyes. It was completely irrational, he knew that. Still, a shudder passed the whole length of his body, and he nodded somberly at her.

"Daddy?"

"What, Sweetie?"

"Can we keep reading?"

Long after she was asleep, he lay awake and thought about it. It was night, he told himself, he was tired, emotionally stirred up, hyper as the kitten he could hear racing around in the bare living room where he'd closed it in for the night. He'd been reading too much of that reincarnation stuff. Who knew about such things?

Maybe he'd just been struck by a resemblance he hadn't noticed before. It was not as if he'd spent a lot of time alone with her. Besides, she was his mother's granddaughter; why wouldn't she look like her?

Or maybe, he decided, maybe he was simply seeing for the first time, soberly and clearly, the kind of look that passes between young children and their parents, and so he identified what he felt then with his mother, recalling a look in her eyes he'd seen when he was little. Yes, that was probably it.

He dozed and thought about his mother's thwarted life, her intelligence, her frustration, her early death. Near morning he came to an understanding: it didn't matter if his mother had ricocheted around on some astral plane until she returned as his daughter. It didn't matter if the moment had been an illusion, a function of being tired and stressed. What mattered was making sure that nothing and no one would hold his daughter back as his mother had been. It was more than personal redemption, amends for his transgressions; it was a chance for the past and future to conjoin and make sense in a way they never had before in his life. It was a promise. A vow.

The tap-bell on the glass counter out in front of the station dinged several times. It was Mrs. Hanley's son, Marshall, come to pick up the Ford. As Walter approached him, the young man removed his headphones and kept them around his neck without turning them off. Walter could hear a tiny band playing heavy metal as Marshall fished out his credit card.

Walter swiped the card and waited while the winged horse on the blue LCD screen over the cash register reared, flapped its wings once, twice, and lifted off, over and over again, looking for all the world as if it was trying and failing to escape from a box. Finally, the printer spit out the ticket, Walter tore and offered it, and Marshall, having determined no interaction was required, placed the headphones back on his ears and signed it.

"The key's in it," Walter said to his back as he walked away.

Time for the VW. The phone rang. Donny again. "Walter? Walter, it's Donny D., I mean, you know, Donny."

"Hi Donny."

"From AA."

"Donny, I'm busy. What can I do for you?"

"I'm in trouble, Walter. I'm in big, big trouble." Walter refused to pump the information from him. He watched the Ford leave the station, fishtailing and peeling rubber.

"Walter?"

"I'm right here, Donny."

"I got served. She fuckin' served me! Gave me a bunch of sweet talk just this week about don't worry, we just need a rest from each other to sort things out and then she fuckin' serves me! Divorce, man. Why am I working so hard to do the right thing, man? What's the point? Who gives a shit?"

"Do you?"

"What?"

"Give a shit?"

"I just want her back, man."

"Donny, look. This is about your drinking. This is not about her or what she said or what you thought she said. This isn't about what she did. It's about what you did. Now you're up against the truth, okay? I hate to sound like a hard-ass, but the main thing is to ride this out and not drink over it."

Silence.

"Donny?"

"Been there. Done that."

"When?"

"Now."

"You're drinking now?"

"I can't just let her walk away like that!" Walter heard a sob.

"Why not? Why can't you?" It was coming clear to Walter, it was what empty men, what men with missing pieces did. He could see it like a diagram of a power train. Woman as missing part: ignition, clutch, voltage regulator, brake. He couldn't put it into words. Sobs on the other end of the line.

"Donny."

"You're pissed at me, aren't you?"

"That's not the question either, Donny. What are you going to do?"

"Nothing."

"Can you get to a meeting?" There was a crash on the other end, Donny saying "Oh, fuck!" away from the receiver, then it sounded like he dropped the phone.

"Donny?" Walter gave it a minute and hung up.

It wasn't until he'd cut away most of the old gasket around the damaged windshield of the VW and started to remove it that Walter became suspicious. He ran his fingers over the glass at the point of impact, the center of the web of brokenness. There was no way, not with the plastic laminate pressed outward like this, that the impact had come from outside the car. He slipped into the driver's seat, extended his right arm toward the windshield. Made a fist. Exactly. He did a little experiment, punched the windshield elsewhere, new cracks radiating outward. The thin skin of plastic casing stretched the same way. He got out of the car, heart pounding, slammed the door hard, and punched the windshield from the outside. He ran his hand over the spot. "Jesus, a baseball," he said out loud, "not a chance, no way."

He worked like a demon, dislodging the windshield with blows from the heel of his hand, ripping out the old rubber gasket, throwing them both in the dumpster. He cleaned and siliconed the metal around the opening and tucked the new gasket in all around. He rigged the wire so that after he'd maneuvered the new windshield into position he could use it to pull the inside lip of the gasket over the metal flange. When he was done, he called Nancy at work.

Out sick. He called her at home.

"Hello?"

"Hello yourself. I called your work and they said you were sick so I called to see how you're doing."

"Oh, hi Daddy. No. I'm fine. I just needed a day to catch up. A mental health day."

"Nancy?"

"What?"

"You'd tell me if you were in trouble, wouldn't you?"

Later on he'd realize that this was the point where, if she didn't know what he was getting at, she would have asked what he was getting at.

"Of course I would."

"Well then. If you talk to Cal, tell him the Bug's done. I'll leave a message at his office. Tell him I'll wait for him here. I want to talk with him."

Next was a Chrysler that needed a new water pump, a Dodge that needed a new ignition and solenoid, new brake pads for a Honda, two drive-in tire repairs, and a muffler and tail pipe assembly for a rusty old Cadillac. All afternoon, as he worked, Walter thought of what he wanted to say to his son-in-law. Clarity came and went, interrupted by waves of anger and sadness and old guilt he thought he'd done with. At five thirty a car dropped Cal off. He wore his briefcase on a strap across his chest. He walked right over to the VW and ran his hand over the new windshield. He flashed Walter a grin and a double thumbs up.

"Looks great!" he said. "Good as new! Thanks, man."

Walter realized the sit-down, the heart-to-heart he'd been imagining all afternoon, was not going to happen. It couldn't. He had been thinking of the young air salesman, of Donny, of himself those many years ago, and he'd wanted to take this boy—oh, that's what he was all right, a boy—take him by the shoulders and somehow make him feel the strength and concern and warning of his scarred hands that understood so much. Then the words might come. Then he would tell him that he understood what it was like to feel adrift, unchallenged, used as badly as this rotten world has always used young men, how it twists and distorts every decent impulse, shames and maims them, shrinks and breaks them. Instead he said, gruffly, walking toward him, "What's my name?"

"What?"

"I have a name. What's my name?" He held the driver's side door of the VW open for him.

"What do you mean?"

"Am I Walter? Dad? Pops? Mr. Crosby? Get in, get in."

Cal's face colored red as he slid into the driver's seat. "I. I don't know. I guess it depends on what you want me to call you."

"No, I would say it depends on how well we understand each other, don't you think?"

Cal nodded and grinned nervously. "I guess."

"I would like to think that I could be a kind of older friend or advisor." Walter squatted next to the VW and through the small open window placed his hand on Cal's shoulder. He was surprised to find his hand shaking, and he thought Cal must surely feel his thumb trembling where it rested at the hollow of his throat. Good, he decided. "I'm good at fixing other things besides windshields is what I'm trying to say."

"I know that."

Walter reached in with his left hand and stroked the inside of the windshield as if to remove a streak or smudge. "But it's easier when people tell me the truth, when I know how things stand." He gave Cal's collarbone a single pat as if in amity or reassurance but let his thumb graze, lightly, the young man's Adam's apple.

Cal squirmed. The paper-tagged key was in the ignition but when he tried to lean forward, Walter tensed his arm and kept him pinned to the back of the seat.

"I was a young man once, a young husband, but not by any stretch a good one. I imagine you've heard that story."

"Yes, yes I have."

"All right. So here is what you need to know—you do with it what you want—you need to know that I remember what it's like to have your rage twist up your way of seeing things, confuse you, twist you so you can't tell friends from enemies. Do you know what I'm trying to say to you?"

"I think so."

"Good. Because I never, ever, want a reason to feel that kind of rage again. We understand each other?" Walter felt Cal swallow.

"Yes, sir."

"Walter. Call me Walter, son." He squeezed Cal's shoulder and withdrew. His stiff knees cracked as he straightened himself up. "I'll go call Nancy, tell her you're on your way."

HARVEY'S BIRTHDAY

Harvey had the habit of running his hand over the bald top of his head when he was nervous. He knew that only drew attention to his baldness, and sometimes he would catch himself doing it and stop. He once thought he might buy a hairpiece, but he'd never seen one that looked real; even when they were the right color, they didn't fit right. He knew a record producer who wore one, and the way it sat there on his head, Harvey half expected him to press a secret button in his pocket and make it whirl around like a slapstick comic's.

Harvey was ashamed of his belly too. Although he hadn't gained a pound in years, his weight had shifted. Some mornings, before he'd eaten, his stomach flat, he'd stand in front of the mirror, running his hand over his crown again and again, thinking that he still looked pretty good when he pulled his shoulders back. But soon after breakfast he became bloated; most days he stayed that way all day, and he took to wearing loose clothing. Awful sounds, like cloth tearing or a chain run through a ring, came from his distended middle; or thunder, as if there were a storm inside the great inflated hollow of himself.

Rick and Linda had invited him upstate from the city to celebrate his fortieth birthday, and walking through the woods to the river with them, Harvey thought how little they had changed in all the years he'd known them. He'd been best man at their wedding in, what was it, 1972? That hadn't been his title, they hadn't given him one, but he had been the one in charge of the rings. It had been an eccentric affair: Rick and Linda, twenty, maybe twenty-two years old, both in white robes, the minister in a paisley dashiki cut in a V down the front to show his clerical collar, dancers in tights attempting to demonstrate the idea of union without being lewd, and here and there a joint being passed around. Who were they then? Just barely adults, all of them, yet Rick and Linda seemed substantial even then, secure, a younger version of this couple he was walking with. Later they moved to L.A., then Vancouver, then Colorado, and now back east to upstate New York.

Rick walked with a folded blanket under one arm, one hand on the bowl of his ever-present, ever-burning pipe, the other holding a book with his forefinger stuck in the pages for a bookmark. Rick was a psychotherapist, but it always seemed to Harvey that the rest of his life was an interruption of his reading.

Linda carried a canvas bag that Harvey figured probably contained her voodoo stuff. He had always called it her voodoo stuff though he meant no disrespect. Although she made her living as a nurse, she had published articles on astrology, tantric yoga, alchemy, and herbal medicine. From time to time she'd send him one, torn from a magazine, with a short note; sometimes all it said was FYI with *X*s and *O*s for a signature.

Harvey had his towel under his arm, rolled as always when he went swimming, but this time there was nothing in it. They were going to a nude beach. Harvey ran his hand repeatedly over the top of his head as they walked.

"Harvey, remember that song you wrote for Sylvia?" said Linda. "The one about, well not about, but the one where you said, 'The woods and water whisper: Eden's here, O Eden's here.' "

"That was the refrain," said Harvey. So they were going to bring up Sylvia. Just like the time he'd visited them out West. Poor Harvey. Marries his perfect partner, singer of his songs, his inspiration, and she up and dies on him. They never knew her. What did they know? Pity. Screw pity.

"Didn't Bonnie Raitt record that?" asked Rick.

"It was never released. Her producer sent me a tape. It's some-where. Packed away. So you remember it?"

"Just that part," said Linda. "I was thinking how this place re-minds me of it. Wait till you see it, Harvey, it's perfect!"

Harvey was remembering. He tried not to. He tried as hard as he tried to hold in his belly. He could feel his insides rumbling. Except for a few memories of their wedding, which were in fact memories of pictures of their wedding—cutting the cake, sitting in the back of the limo together, Sylvia throwing her garter and trying to hit her older sister's upraised hands—he managed not to remember almost all their times together. The trouble was that his hands remembered; his nose and his chest and his belly and his arms remembered. What came back to him was the smell of her hair and skin, the light down on her forearms, the small pink birthmark on her neck, the feel of her earlobe between his lips. He remembered Sylvia, but he could not, or would not, remember places they had been and things they'd done together.

Off to the left, in bright sunlight, children were sliding down the smooth rocks of the fast water where the streambed dropped suddenly, and there were twelve or fifteen people on the pebbled beach, sitting or lying on towels and blankets, reading or talking in twos and threes. The water poured over the rocks where the children played, then widened and became shallower as it passed the beach until it curved out of sight. The stream had cut though a tall hill so that across the water was a wall of clay and rock on top of which the trees, some with roots exposed, leaned out over the edge. It was as if the whole scene were a trench dug with a spade.

Harvey didn't notice any of this. While Linda and Rick spread out their blanket, holding down the corners with their sneakers, Harvey took off his clothes. Would people look at him? Would they note that he was mushroom-white, potbellied, with pimples on his ass? He ran his hand up over his head again and again.

In the hollow dark of Harvey's swollen self there was thunder, and he feared the storm it augured. Sometimes he would shake and lose control of his body, of his ability to concentrate or follow a conversation. At least this time he knew what he was so nervous about, and a part of him even thought that it was silly for him to be so agitated. Though his insides churned and mumbled, he could almost smile at himself. But only almost: he should have taken better care; he should have gotten more exercise; he should have worn a hat when he was young. He would jog; he would get more sunshine; he would write songs again. Harvey thought these things wordlessly and all at once.

Intent on not looking at anyone else, Harvey headed straight for the water and waded in up to his neck. The water was warm and soothing. He paddled around for a short while, then found a place where some underwater rocks made a kind of seat, and he wedged himself in and leaned back with his eyes closed. He did not look back at the beach.

Linda got her tarot deck from her canvas bag. "Read your cards for you, babe?" The smoke from Rick's pipe was a blue the color of spruce.

"Maybe later."

"Does Harvey seem all right to you? I mean I wish he were writing songs again. He says he doesn't think in words anymore. He was good, babe. His songs used to say things, better than most songs I mean."

"I wish he'd gone to see Andrew or Fitz when I referred him."

"But it's been years. What is it now? Ten? Twelve?"

"PTSD," said Rick without looking up from his book.

"Oh come off it babe, he's a friend, not a case."

"It's up to him. It has to be that way."

"It makes you wonder," said Linda. She dealt the cards out on the blanket, for herself.

Harvey lowered himself a little so that only his eyes and nose were out of the water. Like a frog, he thought, I'm like a frog. With my big white belly. Hiding in the water. The part of him that used to be able to laugh at himself smiled just a little. He looked out over the surface of the water. The small swells were different silvers, chrome in the sunlight, a duller nickel color in the shade. The shrieking and laughing of the children was refreshing. In the city, kids ran up and down his block playing, but they yelled "Fuck you!" and "Suck my dick!" at one another. He used to hear them from his studio, before he stopped going there. Besides, it wasn't what everyone thought; the songs had stopped even before Sylvia died. He imagined a short biography, " ... in his youth he wrote several hit tunes." People still spoke of the songs he would write; they would be sad songs, they said, but people love sad songs. But Harvey had written his songs from a place deeper than mere sadness. What was down there where the songs came from was too dark and complicated and tangled. It made noise, not music; it murmured and groaned but did not speak.

Harvey allowed himself a glance at the beach. Linda was playing solitaire; no, probably reading the tarot. Rick was lying on his belly, reading. Harvey looked away, then back. People were keeping pretty much to themselves, to the people assembled in their own small group. One man was sketching. A voyeur in nudist's clothing? Harvey felt the beginning of a laugh, but it was small and only inside himself. A couple were playing chess. He could tell who the regulars were because a few had tanned bottoms, and some of the women's breasts were tanned. He was careful not to gawk. He began to paddle around in the water, ducking his head, taking quick looks.

A tall thin man with white hair walked along the beach; he was wearing a wristwatch. Harvey thought that nothing, not Rick's pipe nor one couple's chessboard, nor the crisp notes of a little radio from somewhere was as hopelessly absurd as this naked old man wearing a watch. He was very tan, all over, with brilliant white hair on his chest. His skin sagged a little, as if it were too big for him, and wrinkled just above the knees and elbows. Harvey ducked under the water, arms along his sides, paddling only with his hands and feet. Like a platypus, he thought. When he surfaced again, he peeked back at the beach. A short, dark-haired woman, her breasts and rump untanned, was asking the old man for the time.

Harvey discovered that if he let all the air out of his lungs, he could get down to the bottom and scrabble along it with his hands for a few seconds like an alligator. When he came up again, there was a loud commotion on the beach.

People were standing, shouting, shaking their fists at someone on the cliff above him. He had to swim back to the beach to see. People were throwing rocks, shouting.

"Pig! Creep! Get out of here!"

Harvey stepped onto the beach and turned to see. On the cliff was a man in a T-shirt and jeans and a baseball cap, looking down at them through binoculars. Right behind Harvey a man yelled, "Go home!" and threw a rock. None of the rocks that people threw reached the intruder, but he vanished back into the dark of the trees.

People muttered their resentment, nodding or shaking their heads at one another. New conversations started. Harvey was offered an apple but turned it down. Looking at everyone and at no one in particular, he walked back to where his clothes lay and stretched out on his towel. The people on the beach were like deer come from the woods to drink, or bear come to fish.

And there was a song coming; not a sad song but a deeply peaceful song, about reassurance and trust and contentment. Harvey borrowed a ballpoint and a used envelope from Rick, lay on his belly, and wrote the first line as it came to him:

When you see we're all the same

Rick and Linda looked at each other with raised eyebrows.

Harvey turned over the envelope and made his first quick list of rhymes:

> blame
> fame
> game
> name
> shame

There was something about this search for rhymes that often started up the musical part of Harvey's imagination. It was going to be a quiet song, but not a sorrowful one. He was just beginning to hear it.

When you see we're all the same

Next he wrote out lines for each of the rhyme words. It was important not to be critical now, to jot whatever came to mind:

> — we are none of us to blame
> — there is no such thing as fame
> — no longer play the game
> — you will be without a name
> — you should never feel ashamed

None of them were what he was after. None led him to the next thought. They were all clichés. Besides, they were all too darkly serious; they were not for the music he was beginning to hear.

Harvey sat up and looked around him, stroking the top of his head. The old man with the watch had a child on his back and was dancing and splashing his feet in the shallow water while the child shrieked with pleasure. Another man stood up and waded into the water. He was overweight but with a very skinny frame so that he appeared to be wearing an umpire's chest protector under his skin, or as if he were an actor who'd stuffed himself with pillows to look more corpulent. A woman on a nearby blanket had a T-shirt on, her shoulders shielded from the sun—but what about her bottom?

A man with thick dark hair on his back and shoulders sat with his arms around his knees next to a large, soft-looking woman lying on her back with her breasts flopped to either side, her flat brown nipples large as campaign buttons. There was a gray-haired woman whose flesh hung down under her arms and at the backs of her knees.

Harvey was losing the song. Where only a few moments ago the only individuals on the beach were Rick and Linda, because he knew them, and the old man, because of the watch, now each one he saw was different from every other, unique and separate. He stroked the top of his head several times and clenched his teeth. His stomach grumbled. He made a pillow from his clothing, leaned back, and tried to regain the feeling he'd had, the snatch of melody he'd almost heard. He went down inside himself and hurt was there, and shame, and fear, all tangled together so that he wanted to open his eyes.

He found that by opening his lids the slightest bit, he could see while still appearing to be napping. The sun on his eyelashes made an iridescent veil of shimmering green and gold, and from behind this veil he watched. There was a short black man with high hips and thin legs with their calves very bunchy and high. A woman off to his left, very pale and with prominent blue veins on the backs of her legs, was kneeling and running a brush through her long red hair. A man was rubbing suntan lotion on a woman's buttocks and back. Harvey began to feel more at ease. He tried again to regain the feeling of the song or at least to feel the beginning of the urge, but he couldn't. He closed his eyes and rested.

Linda was laughing. "Harvey!" And before he knew it, she'd put her hand around the shaft of his penis and slapped the top of it with her other hand. His erection subsided immediately. He got to his feet and ran his hand back over his baldness and looked at her.

"It's okay, Harvey. Hey, don't get embarrassed. It happens to my patients all the time. That's what we do and it goes away. No need to get uptight about it. Harvey?"

Harvey looked around, blinking. The old man with the watch was looking at him, but he immediately turned away.

"I was asleep. Dreaming."

"Some dream!" laughed Linda and reached to take his hand. Rick was grinning at him.

"I'm going to take a walk."

"Calm down."

"I'm going to take a walk, that's all. Okay?" He tried to fasten his towel around him but his waist was too big; he held the ends together with one hand and walked away.

"He'll be all right," said Rick.

Linda watched Harvey walk into the woods, then she turned to Rick and smiled. "I was thinking. There's that part in *The Book of the Dead* where you go through this kind of zone, the last one you go through, where all these naked people are writhing around, and if you get turned on, you get sent back and have to go through life all over again."

"You're thinking Harvey'd never make it," Rick said, and they both laughed.

Harvey found a path along the edge of the woods and followed the river upstream, walking hard. He was shaking. He could hear the fast water and the children's voices behind him for a while then the ground rose and the river fell away beneath him. He stopped and leaned against a tree to catch his breath, but he didn't feel any calmer. He hit the tree with his fist, hard, and tore open his knuckles. He put them to his mouth.

There were voices from the river. He walked to the edge and looked down. There were twelve or fifteen people dressed in dark clothing standing on the fen where the river flowed slowly. Some were getting into a rowboat. He stood behind a tree and watched.

Two men in dark suits rowed the boat out to the middle of the river. There were two women and a young boy in the boat also. Some of the people on the fen were holding one another. Some had their faces in their hands. One man in the boat dropped a small anchor over the stern while the other took out what looked like a shoebox. He lifted the lid and unfolded some purple cloth; then, with a shiny spoon, he began to scatter ashes on the water.

One of the women on the fen looked up and, grabbing the elbow of the man next to her, pointed at Harvey. Harvey stepped back, dropped his towel, stumbled, and fell into a bed of ferns. When he got up, he saw that others were looking up at him. He turned and began to run back along the path to the beach, holding his arms in front of his face to fend off the branches. At every step he said, "*Mmmmm*," in a kind of clenched moan. "*Mmmmm, mmmmm, mmmmm.*" He ran to get back to the beach. Everyone had to get out of the water! Everyone had to get dressed and leave! Who would help him? Rick. No. Linda. No. The old man with the watch! The old man. He would help.

As he ran he thought of children, of the boy in the boat, of the children screeching and laughing and sliding down the slippery rocks, of the kids on the block at home, obscene, alive, and innocent. He thought of Rick with his pipe and books, of Linda with her charts and diagrams and cards, of old women with flat sagging breasts and thin hair, of men with hair all over their backs and chests and arms, of men with binoculars who could not bear to understand what he was understanding. He thought of himself, of his fear, of his fatness and baldness and shame, and of his grief. He thought of Sylvia.

He ran through the woods. He was running past all the places he and Sylvia had been together, past the theater on West End Avenue, past the corner luncheonette, past the vegetable stand, past the Quincy Market in Boston, past Harvard Square in Cambridge, past the farmhouse in Ohio where her parents lived, past Buckingham Palace, past Mount Desert Island, Maine, past the Hotel Centenario in Guatemala City, past, "*Mmmmm*," past, "*Mmmmm*," past, "*Mmmmm.*"

He fell on his hands and knees on the beach and cried. Linda put her arms around him and looked at Rick for help. Harvey cried convulsively, trying to regain control. Some people gathered around to look. Harvey reared back with his hands full of stones, and the people backed away. He lifted his hands and let the stones roll out of them and knelt there, his face in his hands, sobbing. Rick helped Linda get him to his feet.

"Come on, let's get you away from here."

Harvey looked at him. Rick's eyes were full of pity. Screw pity. Through his burning eyes, he looked at the others. Pity. So screw them too. His eyes found the old man's and he found he could meet his gaze without shame.

He turned to Rick. "Okay," he said. He looked around at the others. "It's all right," he said. "Everything's all right."

GUY GOES INTO A THERAPIST'S OFFICE

First thing he sees are several framed certificates on the walls. One looks just like the ad for Renaissance Roofing & Siding (Gutters Our Specialty) that had come in the morning mail. "Fully licensed and insured!" it said. Like the ad, they all have gold seals and signatures at the bottom.
"How can I help?" asks the therapist.
"I'm a bad man," says Guy. "At least I think I am."
"What do your friends think?"
"Friends?"
"I see," says the therapist. "Come back next week."

Next week comes round and Guy notices some changes. The therapist has new furniture. A new rug. New lamps. As he sits in the leather chair it makes a sound of escaping air, almost like a whoopee cushion if whoopee cushions had a wider range and could mime the sounds of the more common, less theatrical fricatives. Guy worries the therapist will think he passed gas. He stands as if to adjust the crease in his trousers and sits again, deliberately hard, to produce a loud whoosh of air that unmistakably comes from the chair cushion. He sees over the therapist's shoulder that there is a new certificate on the wall.
"How are we today?" the therapist asks.
"I'm sad," says Guy, "I don't know about you."
"Yes, you seem agitated. What's going on?"
"Everything and everyone but me it seems."

"Do I detect a note of self-pity?"

Over the therapist's shoulder Guy is trying to read the new framed document. He feels certain he can make out the words "patios" and "driveways".

"I guess I'm not hiding it very well, am I?" says Guy.

The following week the therapist scribbles a prescription. He leans forward and hands it to Guy.

"What's this supposed to do?"

"You wore out your wanter, you wanker."

"What?"

"Your wanter, man, your wisher, your will. The burner's busted. Here. We'll start with a low dose, build up gradually."

"Build up to what?"

"You tell me when you're able to give two shits, and we'll level off from there."

"What's this got to do with my problems?" asks Guy. "I thought we were going to talk about, you know, my childhood. My divorce. I don't know." He squints at the framed document behind the therapist. "Custom cornices" can't be right. And why would it say "asphalt, slate, and rubber"?

"Why are you always harping on the past? What about the future?" asks the therapist.

"Oh," Guy says, "the future. Yeah. That didn't turn out too good either."

SUGAR

We're in the check-out line and I'm putting the groceries on the counter. This is the hardest part of shopping with a two-year-old. Jeffrey's apple, healthful consolation for all the things I have refused him, is down to the core, and he's working himself up to a crescendo of desire. "Daddy, I want a–a– I wants a– a ..."

The narrow passage is walled with mints, gum, lollipops and candy bars. I manage to convince him that it's all yucky, bad for him, that it will give him a tummyache, all the while feeling like a hypocrite because since I quit smoking I always have some gum or candy in my pocket. Then he turns to the film, batteries, cigarettes, and tabloids. I explain to him that cigarettes are also yucky. A headline reads: "Man With Split Personality Weds Self." The woman ahead of us pushes our groceries back with her forearm, tumbling stacked cans, and whacks a wooden stick between our orders. When Jeffrey grabs a bag of disposable razors, I take it from him. He squeezes shut his eyes, his face gets red, and he howls.

Four bags. Sixty dollars. I write the check.

Today, because he is still howling, we make it past the dozen inverted jars of twenty-five-cent jawbreakers, Super Balls, tin rings, stale peanuts, and Slime in plastic bubbles.

"Watch!" I say. "A magic door!" It hums open. Jeffrey yells, "Magic!" and we're outside.

"I want the pony!"

I love this part. The look on his face is a plea but a confident one. I've never refused him. I remember giving my own father that expectant look; and when I dig down deep in my pocket past the car keys and the secret candy, I am my father; and when I lift him under his arms, I can feel my father pick me up and swing me briefly through the air; and when he's in the saddle and I've dropped a quarter in the slot, and the pony bucks and begins to rock, and I see his face first fearful then delighted, I am my son.

I put him in the saddle, worried as always that he'll fall off, and I wonder why the stirrups are so low that by the time your legs are long enough to reach them you're too old to ride. "Hold on tight now."

But this time the quarter drops and nothing happens.

"The pony not go!"

The pony's tail has been bobbed by vandals or just by kids playing hard, but there's a knob of it left for me to grip and rock the pony back and forth. It's hard for me to reach both Jeffrey to steady him and the pony's tail to rock it hard enough to convince him everything is okay. "Watch where you're going!" I tell him when he grows suspicious and starts to turn around. When my shoulder starts to hurt, I tell him to say, "Whoa!" When I lift him down he says, "Thank you, pony."

He doesn't want to sit in the shopping cart. "Then you must hold Daddy's hand," I say. "There are too many cars." The parking lot is jammed: cars are circling, looking for spaces; horns are blowing; people pushing carts are trying to navigate among the cars. I change my mind, lift Jeffrey up and put him in the seat, ignoring his protests.

"Sir! Sir!" A short fat man in a white V-neck T-shirt is coming toward us, one finger held up before him. "You mind if we follow you and grab your cart? There's none left." A boy is with him, about ten or eleven, also fat.

The four of us enter the chaos and make it to the car. When I've loaded the bags, the man thanks me, and the boy takes the cart. I carry Jeffrey, quiet now, around to the other side to buckle him in his car seat.

"Whoa! Whoa! Whoa!" The fat man is yelling at a large red Mercury backing toward the boy who's standing frozen with the shopping cart. The windows on the Mercury are down, and the music is loud. The car is shining; even the tailpipes are polished. It stops, rocking; the driver has slammed the brake.

"Hey! Who the hell you think you're talking to?" The driver, a lean young man in tight black jeans, no shirt, is out of his car and moving toward the fat man.

"I just didn't want you to hit my son, that's all."

The boy stands still with the cart and watches. The young man, even with the boy's father now, puts one hand on his chest and shoves him against the car beside mine, bending him backward over the hood. "What else you got to say to me, huh? You got a big mouth. What else you got to say to me?"

The man, his hands crossed in front of his frightened face, says, "Nothing. I'm sorry. Sorry."

I see the boy turn away. He doesn't move, just stands there with the cart until the shirtless man gets back in his gleaming car, slams the door, and revs the engine. I see the father catch up to the boy and put his hand on his son's shoulder and the boy shrug off his touch and walk ahead very fast, fat jiggling, pushing the cart, wiping his eyes with the back of his hand. I see myself, having done nothing, not doing anything, and not saying anything now to the heavy man who stands still, looking down, before he follows after his son.

While I buckle the belts of his car seat, Jeffrey asks me, "Why that man was shouting?"

"I don't know, Jeffrey." I walk around and get in the driver's seat.

"Daddy, why that man was shouting?"

"Because he's angry."

"Why?"

"I don't know."

"Why?"

"I don't know, Jeffrey, I don't know why the man is angry."

"But why you don't know?"

"Because I don't, that's why!" I shout at the ceiling. I start the engine and release the brake.

Jeffrey is screaming now, and when I turn, angry and out of patience, and see his face, I know this is not a tantrum. Tears pour from his eyes and his face is white with fear. I pull the brake back on, lean back, and touch him.

"Daddy's sorry. Don't cry. Daddy's sorry. Wait," I say, "I have something good for you." I push myself up high in the seat so I can reach down deep in my pocket.

BURNING BRIGHT

Soon after he turned four, Roger surprised his parents by asking them if it was fun to die. His father hesitated. His mother said to him, "Well, what do you think?"

Roger stood at the bottom of the stairs, hugging the newel post. He shrugged. Then he asked them who was going to die.

His parents, when they looked at each other, passed back and forth what each hoped the other would read as amusement and pride, but each had felt, and hidden, a chill.

"Well, Big Guy, everybody has to die sometime," the boy's father said, kneeling close to the child. But this time when he looked at his wife, looked to her for some help, he saw that he'd annoyed her. "What's with the look?" he wanted to say, "What am I supposed to tell him?"

But it had been the tone of her husband's remark, his manner more than the substance of his reply, that had irked the child's mother. He had made a hard truth even harder somehow, as if with a cheery inflection and a wave of the hand even this mystery of mysteries was solved. She had heard this tone in his voice before, on the phone, responding to a customer's difficult question. "Clients," he called them. She felt alarmed in ways she didn't fully understand yet. What was he selling the child then? Did he even know? Of course he was talking again, a little too rapidly, with the air of one expanding on his main point, though he wasn't, really.

" … and your mother and I are both healthy and young. Is that what you're worried about? You don't need to worry about that, Mr. Big, not for a minute, you hear?"

She kept her face turned from her husband so the child wouldn't have to see her hesitate when his father looked to her for agreement. She looked straight at the child and could tell by the way he shifted his gaze that she'd been wise to do so. She tried to radiate a general reassurance and strength, to focus it like a ray and beam it at the child's face.

This was disturbing. It was all wrong what her husband seemed to be saying. She felt such a fundamental revulsion to his voice that, right there in front of the child, she wanted to scream at him to shut up. She felt that her child was being hustled and silenced, fooled and numbed. A response was required, but for now she could only acknowledge her anger and, for the child's sake, hide it. Partly, she was simply too disturbed to speak, at a loss and grievously astonished. Without knowing precisely why, she understood that all that had seemed substantial now threatened to unravel.

The boy looked back at his father who winked, patted him on the cheek, and stood up. He watched his father turn to his mother with no look on his face, none, nothing, and walk right past her and out the front door. The boy thought this was odd because they only ever used the front door when people rang the bell; otherwise, they used the back and went in and out through the kitchen.

His mother knelt, on both knees, and hugged him. She didn't speak. Sometimes she did this — squeezed him a little too hard. It was like the times his father clamped his thumb and finger on his chin to make him pay attention. Then he wanted to get away, go dig in the dirt or draw a picture. She released him and he ran upstairs.

Earlier that morning, the garage had called to say that the Toyota was ready. They'd planned on driving there together so one of them could drive it back, but Russell was out of the driveway and headed there in the company car before he realized he had decided to pick it up himself. He wasn't sure how, but he'd figure it out when he got there. There would be a thick rope or a chain or something he could borrow from the garage. It wasn't far. He let out his anger in the solitude of the car, speaking to his wife as if she were there in the passenger seat, holding up his index finger to make a point or chopping the air with his right hand for emphasis.

"You don't just abandon the poor kid to his own devices with shit like, 'I don't know. What do you think?' You don't give a good goddamn what the boy thinks, and he knows it. Besides, he asked because he'd reached the limit of his understanding. When else does a boy ask a question like that? Tell me. I don't think you understand about boys. Maybe that stuff works with girls. I don't pretend to know. I just don't think you understand about boys.

"Of course! Of course you have the right to say anything you want to him. Of course he's your son, too." He was hitting the steering wheel with the heel of his hand. "So say something to him is all I'm saying. Don't duck with these child psychology tricks you learned in teacher's ed. I respect him as a little man, that's the difference. You don't respect him."

He kept his eyes on the road and refrained from gesticulating as he approached an intersection where a panel truck was waiting for him to pass. In the rearview mirror he watched the truck turn and go in the other direction. He turned his attention back to the ghost of his wife, but felt too self-conscious now to continue. He hoped there would be a length of chain and maybe an old tire to put between the two bumpers. That would work. Leave a little slack in the chain so he could make the turns, and fasten an old tire to the rear bumper of the tow car to protect both cars on the way back. His anger dissipated as his plan took shape.

He slowed and pulled into the service station. The Toyota was parked outside the repair bay, with one mechanic leaning under the hood, giving hand signals to another who sat behind the steering wheel with the door open and one foot on the ground, occasionally gunning the engine.

Now what, he thought. I thought they said the car was ready.

Beth sat in the bright dining room where the shadows of potted palm and ficus emphasized the morning sun, but she couldn't think there, and she couldn't sit still. She needed to walk to think, but with Roger upstairs in his room and Russell gone god knows where, she was trapped.

She went in the kitchen and lit the burner under the kettle, but as soon as she lifted a tea bag from the canister she changed her mind, put the lid back on, whirled around, and turned off the stove. She couldn't find a way to start to think about what had just happened. She had seen how profoundly different she and her husband were, and it frightened her.

She stood looking out the windows above the sink at the sugar maple in the side yard next to the driveway. Once before, when the world had seemed to spin madly out of orbit, threatening to fling her from sanity, to dislodge her by the centripetal force of grief, she had hugged that maple and held on. Now she filled a small plastic tumbler from the faucet and watered the African violets and geranium on the windowsill, staring out at the tree and remembering.

It had been right around the time that she'd weaned Roger, hoping it wasn't too early to do so, and feeling alternately guilty and resolute about it, just as she had while he was nursing: one moment he was so serene he'd fall asleep at the nipple, the next he was biting down so hard she almost slapped him, reflexively. "No!" she would exclaim then, through sudden tears, and detach herself, ashamed of how angry she felt, but damned if she was going to be "gnawed upon," as she put it to her husband.

On that day three years ago, when her husband came to tell her of her brother Jerry's death, she had just returned from a walk, a habit she'd acquired while pregnant; "my walk," she called it, marveling that although the route was always the same, the walk, her walk, was always different. The season, the weather, the light, her mood, her outlook, her expectations for later in the day — any number of variables combined to make her every circular walk trailblazing and unprecedented. Some days, where the road curved past the fenced meadow, just before she came upon the broad pond, cows would drift down the hill to the fence to greet her; other times she would round the curve to see the whole herd near the fence, and then they would walk away as if they'd all agreed, earlier, to shun her. Now her walks were tethered in her mind to her brother because of the happenstance of her hearing the news there, in the side yard, under the sugar maple, as she returned home.

She had seen her husband coming toward her, and she smiled and walked a few steps farther before she stopped and touched her hand to the tree. He was walking toward her with a resolve that suggested he might walk right past her and keep on going to somewhere far away, as if he were hiking, reluctantly but resolutely. Very nearly marching, it had occurred to her, and by the time he drew near enough for her to see his face, she already knew something was terribly wrong, and knew that it wasn't the baby since there was no panic in his movement. Days later she would shoo away the thought, and more than once, that she had seen mostly impatience on his face, a man who had to clean up a mess and had better things to do.

She couldn't remember how he'd first touched her. Had he put his arms around her before or after he'd told her? Which one of them moved first? Had she sought comfort from him? Did he hold her head to his chest, a habit of his that she felt infantilized her, and was that why she turned away and leaned into the tree? He had stayed there with her until she was ready to go inside, not speaking, not touching her. What she remembered was that the way he had held her, and let her go, and stood by in silence, was not at all the way she would have imagined things should be, but that it had sufficed. She had turned to the tree, leaned her forehead into the trunk, and wept. When the anger took over, she grabbed the thick trunk and wailed, trying over and over to shake the tree but it wouldn't budge. Soon she had her arms around it, like a fighter tying up an opponent to catch a breath, and then she slid to the ground and sat there hugging the tree with her arms and legs, convinced that if she let go she would hurtle from the earth into nothing but the purest pain.

And then her menses had returned. At first she hadn't been aware of it, subsumed in grief and melded to the tree, but soon it was wet and warm and undeniable, although she could, and did, choose to ignore it. She continued crying, scraping her cheeks and forehead on the bark, until she felt her equilibrium returning; she fought it, not ready yet to turn back to the world where brothers die, preferring her own disappearance into the roaring white water of grief. But no more tears would come.

Instead, as she rose and turned to her husband, who had stood there, who had stood by her there, and with profound reluctance prepared to shoulder her identity again, the early October wind came up without warning and shook the yellowing tree so that it pitched and rocked and yellow leaves were blown from it and flew off sideways until they stuck to a fence or wall.

Whether a tree can speak or not is not the issue, she tried to tell her husband later on. What she'd heard then, in the loud whisperings of the maple's windblown crown, was the knowledge that each single moment is essential to every other, that if it were not, then no one, ever, would have to die. What she understood then, that the fact of dying proves the necessity of each and every moment to every other that has ever existed or ever will exist, filled her with such peace that her brother's death, which hurt more than anything she had ever known, became acceptable to her. She tried, over the next several weeks, to make her husband understand until one evening he finally turned to her and said, "Enough. I'm thick. Okay? I just don't get it. Save your breath."

In his room the boy was on his knees and drawing on a piece

of posterboard with an orange crayon. When he pressed too hard and broke it, he said, "Good!" in a voice that was not yet his own. Peeling back the paper wrapper, exposing the jagged edge, he said it again, "Good!" And he bore down with the crayon — sharp dark lines now over the lighter pebbled orange. He thought this might be fire he was drawing. If he had to say — if someone, a grown-up, would ask him in the grown-up singing voice that always prompted him to answer — he would have said, "Fire," wishing for them to go away and, as if he had paid them, satisfied them somehow, they would.

The brown crayon. Then the yellow one. The black crayon was in pieces. He picked up one so rounded, paperless, and slick it might have been a jellybean. "Good!" he said. It should have black on it but not too much.

As he worked on his picture, he was thinking. Just as he brought things to his room to know them, to interrogate them — horse chestnuts, certain rocks, an elbow of pipe, a spiky partly opened milkweed pod — he brought what happened, what he had observed. His four-year-old self had a pocket in it. Yellow and red will make a better orange than orange. Those are not flames. Those are ears. Green all around is important. He thought while the picture became. He became, wholly, the boy who was making this picture.

"Happens sometimes. Can't tell until you go to start the bugger up again. Sometimes the ignition wires get brittle so when you hook them up again you find out they're shot." The mechanic lowered the hood, then dropped it. Bang. He walked toward Russell, wiping his hands on a rag. "Take about an hour. You can wait inside or come back. Up to you."

Having to wait was irritating and returned Russell to the argument with his wife. The grimy tubular steel chair in the office was uncomfortable. It occurred to him that this was almost a religious difference, if there could be such a thing between non-believers.

He had married a fellow atheist and found himself in a mixed marriage. The irony didn't wake his sense of humor, though; on the contrary, he felt a wave of panic pass through him, the perception of how complicated and beyond governing was this thing called marriage.

He had no patience for what seemed to him to be her facile, hippie wisdom. He'd seen this delusion before, the first time during a rocket attack in the Central Highlands. Ordnance flying everywhere: screaming shells, screaming soldiers. And one of them, a kid named Scott, sitting on the tarmac on the edge of the compound babbling about transcending fear. Raving. Laughing at death. Making life thus inconsequential. Bullshit. It was a dodge, that's what it was. Despair with a happy face stuck on it. He lived, the kid, rotated out. He should have been busted, the little prick.

So if she needed to make believe she'd grasped something fucking ineffable, fine; but he had no intention of being drawn in or letting her warp the boy for that matter.

He looked out the window across the station at the traffic going by. A lot of trucks this time of day. He remembered Roger in his arms just moments after he was born, and how he had hummed "Old Man River" to him in his deepest voice, surprising himself, not knowing he was going to do it, with his chin against the infant's skull. Pouring into this act all his sorrow, joy, grief, anger: aggregates of that same ghost he had given up in drunken song, from the bottom of illness, in the moan of the love bed, so many times before, but now at last his own to give, this ghost that could only be known in transmission, that did not depend on the words of the song, but only on the love with which he shaped each vowel in his deepest belly-voice.

The mechanic was there in the doorway. "She's ready. What's the trouble with the other one?" He nodded toward the Taurus Russell had arrived in.

"That one? Nothing. Company car."

The mechanic frowned. "I thought you come to pick her up."

"I did. I did. I'm wondering if you have an old tire and a length of chain. Or a good strong rope would probably do the trick."

"You're shittin' me, right? You want to tow it home with a piece of rope?"

"Why not? It's not far."

"Not out of here you're not."

Challenged, Russell felt a surge of anger. It was his car, after all. Even the company car was his, really, since he owned the company. He looked the mechanic up and down. Banty rooster on his own turf. "Give me one good reason."

"'Cause I won't let you. You'll bang up both these cars but good. And that's if you don't kill yourself and take somebody else down with you. What's the matter with you? You got some kind of death wish?"

He turned and opened the door to a storage closet next to the shelves of motor oil and antifreeze. In the time it took the mechanic to open the lid on a can of hand cleanser and scoop two fingers of it into his palm, Russell got a good look at a large photograph on the inside of the door. Above the picture of a large group of men in combat fatigues was a sign, in stenciled letter, reading:

2nd Battalion, 4th Marines

There were other regalia as well, but the mechanic closed the door before Russell got much of a look. The strong but pleasant scent of citrus cleaner filled the grimy office.

"You're a bastard," Russell said.

"I can be."

"A magnificent bastard — that's what we called you guys."

"Who's we?"

"Gimlet. Americal. 3rd Battalion, 21st Infantry. Russell Hartshorne." He put out his hand. "Nhi Ha."

"Ernie Gagnon." He took Russell's hand and held on. "So, shall I save your sorry ass or you still want to fight me?" Russell waited for the smile that would defuse this moment; when it came he gave Gagnon's hand a quick pump and they both let go.

"So what's the plan?" asked Russell.

Beth took her old textbook from the low shelf on the upstairs landing and sat in a creaking white wicker chair by the window. Were all four-year-olds interested in death? Was this a developmental thing? Or was Roger speaking from a chill shadow his uncle's death had cast over their family life? Beth sought the answer to the first question in the heavy maroon volume on her lap. She feared the answer to the second.

Nothing in the index for death. Nothing for mortality. Nothing for mourning. Nothing for grief. Did the authors think none of these things were of any consequence in a child's life? The listing for parent was extensive. There: bereaved parent, page 437. Dry as ashes, the text referred to "the maternal introject" and the danger to a child of "overwhelming affect" resulting from "acute maternal bereavement."

She refused the guilt that welled up in her and slammed shut the book. Tears came then, this time at the realization that there was nothing to be done, nothing that ought to be done, nothing that could be changed. She cried for Jerry, for his final moments; for Roger who seemed to have perceived her brother's absence, even without really knowing him; for Russell, for whom death, anybody's death, was a kind of failure, a collapse into incoherence; and for herself, facing mystery brotherless.

She heard cars in the driveway and went to the window. A mechanic in coveralls was working a tow truck's lift, lowering the front end of the Toyota to the ground.

"No, I told you. No charge."

"Well, you got my business for a lifetime."

Gagnon cocked his head and looked at Russell. He kept his hand on the hydraulic lever until the bar, chain, and canvas apron clanked back in place on the truck. "That was my brother," he said. "My brother's outfit, Fourth Marines. Not mine."

"The stuff in the closet."

"Yeah. All the stuff he sent me before he didn't come back."

"I'm sorry."

Gagnon was climbing into the cab now. "Didn't want to leave you with the wrong impression is all. That wouldn't be right." He gunned the truck in reverse, swinging into the street. He shifted and took off, acknowledging Russell's raised hand with a quick wave, eyes straight ahead.

Roger had watched from his bedroom window where he could see the tow truck turn at the corner and pass from view. He returned to his picture, anxious to finish now. Along the left margin he made a row of mountains. He had never seen real mountains, but in his picture book they seemed like the edge of things, the limit, so he turned his paper to draw another set of jagged peaks along the right-hand side.

Holding his picture in both hands, he sat on the top stair, and he made his way down, sitting on each step, by using his feet. His parents were in the kitchen, hugging, just inside the back door. His mother turned to him; he could see she had been crying.

"What you got there, Big Guy?" his father boomed.

Roger held his picture out in front of him: an animal, orange and black with long lines for legs, stiltlike, resembling an insect, and with saw-toothed jaws depicted full front though the drawing was in profile. A creature horrific and improbable, protected on either side by purple mountains.

"Tiger!" Roger instructed them. Then he dropped his drawing and, leaning forward, arms locked at his sides and ending in fists, he roared at the both of them.

GUY GOES INTO A BARBERSHOP

The barber looks up from his customer and nods. Guy touches his right eyebrow with his index finger in a little salute, hangs his jacket and hat on a hook, and turns to a stack of magazines: Agni, Hudson Review, The New Yorker, New York Review of Books, Paris Review, The American Scholar. *No* Field & Stream? *No* Argosy, Popular Mechanics, Maxim, Esquire, GQ? *But the barber's shaking out the striped cape and it's his turn in the chair.*

"How goes it?" *asks the barber.*

"Can't complain," *says Guy.*

"Ah! Never complain and never explain," *chirps the barber.*

Guy watches him in the mirror, his movements, his assured manner. He looks at the barber's instruments on the marble counter and in various holsters hanging below it.

"So what's it gonna be?"

"Just trim the sides and back. Go easy on the top. There's not a whole lot left up there, y'know?" *He grins at the barber in the mirror.*

"Hopes dance best on bald men's hair!" *says the barber.*

"Come again?"

"Hope. You know, the thing with feathers that perches in the soul."

"Oh. Yeah. Yeah. And I could use a shave."

"That's an extra two bucks with the haircut. Costly thy habit as thy purse can buy!"

"That's reasonable."

"The reasonable man adapts himself to the world: the unreasonable one persists in trying to adapt the world to himself. Therefore all progress depends on the unreasonable man."

"I never quite thought about it that way," Guy says and grows wary. Mostly he hopes this isn't one of those barbers who doesn't care if he gets those little hairs all down your neck so you itch the whole rest of the day. He closes his eyes and listens to the scissors do their work.

"Mind if I ask you something?" the barber says.

"No. Go ahead."

"Well, if there were no eternal consciousness in a man, if at the foundation of all there lay only a wild seething power which writhing with obscure passions produced everything that is great and everything that is insignificant, if a bottomless void never satiated lay hidden beneath all — what then would life be but despair?"

"Damned if I know," says Guy.

Soon the barber is holding his jaw shut, scraping at his neck. "Every normal man," the barber says, "must be tempted at times to spit on his hands, hoist the black flag, and begin to slit throats."

With this, Guy sits up. "Are you nuts? Is that it? I'm not going to sit here scared half to death while you hold a razor to my throat."

"Fear not that thy life shall come to an end, but rather fear that it shall never have a beginning," the barber says as he smacks Guy on the cheeks with something that stings and smells like lime. "Relax," he says.

"How can I relax with you talking like that?"

"Let people see in what I borrow whether I have known how to choose what would enhance my theme. For I make others say what I cannot say so well, now through the weakness of my language, now through the weakness of my understanding."

Then the barber holds up the hand mirror behind Guy's head — a bogus lollipop, an all-day sucker, paddle of a clown. "Give me to know the measure of my days," he says.

Guy sees in the mirror before him the long approach of himself and he is afraid to meet his eyes for fear the whole train, on the thin, black, twin track of his pupils, will come screeching to a halt inside the brilliant

station of his head. But he can also see, in the mirror the barber holds,
that he has already emerged from his cerebrations intact, already turned
toward the future, behind him that is, and away from what is now, today,
staring him right in the face.

The barber is already sweeping up as Guy gets to his feet and fumbles
in his wallet. The barber, about to sweep the gathered pile into a long-
handled dustpan, sees Guy's quizzical look when he notices the several
numbers swept into a pile with the hair.

"Footnotes," the barber says.

LUCKY GARDEN

In a Chinese restaurant a block up the hill from the high school, the kind with a green and yellow neon dragon in the window, a beaded curtain in the entry and booths along the walls, a young man in the dress uniform of the Marine Corps, several rows of ribbons above his heart, sat with his white hat and gloves on the seat next to him, across from a young African American woman. With just a hint of Latin America in his voice, he asked her if she had brought the papers with her.

"I have them here, all filled out." She took a manila envelope from her school bag.

The Marine looked at the menu, a laminated card. "That's good. That's good. So. Let's order first, okay? I'm starving. You hungry? I could go for a nice big pupu platter."

The young woman continued to hold out the envelope to him. "I want to be able to fly. To any place I want to go."

"I don't see no pupu platter here. Do you?"

She withdrew the envelope, holding it beside her face. "I don't know," she said. "I don't know what that is."

"Don't worry. You can fly to all kinds of places for free. So long as there is a plane going there and they have room, you can get on it. To anywhere you want."

"No, I mean can I fly the plane? I want to fly planes." She set the envelope aside.

"You want to fly them?"

"Yeah, fly them."

"Well, you have to be an officer."

"How do I become an officer?"

"You have to have a degree."

"You mean like college? Four years?"

"I think that in the Corps you can get a degree in three years. I have to check it out, though. What do you like to eat? You would like the pupu platter. I don't see no pupu platter on the menu, but I bet they have it."

The young woman turned the menu back and forth as if it were hopeless. "I don't know," she said. "I'll have the egg drop soup."

"You never had a pupu platter? Girl, you don't know what you're missing."

"I just want soup."

"But what about some food? You know? Real food? A Marine can't live on soup."

"I'm not a Marine."

"We'll get to that. You have to start building yourself up."

"That's all I want right now. When I get home, I'm going to sit in front of TV, pig out, and do my homework."

"That's good. Homework's good. You got to get good grades. Especially if you want to try for officer."

"What about medical school?"

"Medical school!" He sniffed, frowned, and looked down at the menu. "If they don't have the pupu platter, I'll get moo goo gai pan."

"What?"

"It's like a kind of chicken. It has pea pods and other vegetables and stuff. You would like it. Why don't you get some?"

"I'm good with the soup. So if I want to go to med school will you help me?"

"I thought you wanted to be a pilot."

"I told you before. I was thinking I could be a doctor who flies to places, wherever, you know, like where people are sick."

"I'm going to have to check on that. But I think you can. As long as you pass all the tests and like that."

"What tests?"

"Whatever. There's a test for everything. Like I said, I'll check it out for you."

The waiter, an old man in baggy khakis and a white shirt, had shuffled over to the booth.

"You have pupu platter?" the Marine asked him.

The waiter took the menu from the table, looked it over, shook his head. "No. You need more time?"

"No no. This young lady here is going to have the egg drop soup. I want moo goo gai pan. Number *L*, uh, eleven. With chicken fingers and fried rice. That's it."

The waiter went away.

"What are you?" asked the young woman.

"Huh?"

"What year were you born?" She reached across and pointed to his placemat. "You can look up whether you're a pig or a rat or a monkey or a dragon."

"That don't make sense. If everybody born the same year is the same thing then that can't be right."

"What year?"

"I was born in 1981. But I don't believe this stuff. Besides, already I been all these things. Except the chicken."

"Rooster, that's a rooster. Look, that's you, 1981. You're a rooster!"

"Then okay! Okay by me!" He puffed his chest out and jutted his chin and they both laughed. "What are you? You're eighteen, right? That makes you, what?" He looked at the placemat. "A horse! *Una potra!*"

"What? What did you call me?"

"It's nothing bad. Means a young girl horse."

"I guess if you have to be a chicken, I can handle being a girl horse."

"Rooster!"

She smiled at him and shook her head.

"Okay, so let's look at your papers," he said.

She took them from a manila envelope and handed them across to him.

"What did you write for why you want to join?"

"I wasn't sure what to write."

"Wait. Oh, man. Why you want to go and write 'My uncle tried to choke me'? That's not a good thing to say. You have to say why you want to join."

"I'm sorry."

"You have to be positive, girl. Who needs to know that? Why you want to go and say that? That's not going to help you."

"You told me to write the truth."

He looked up from reading the folder. "And your mom has cancer? When they see that they are definitely not going to let you in."

"Why not?"

"They'll think that maybe you're running away from home or something. The Marines don't want no runaways. Maybe they'll think that you should be at home and taking care of your mother, you ever think about that?"

"Is that what you think?"

"That don't make no difference what I think."

"But do you? Because by the time I'm all joined up, my mother will be gone. She don't have long now."

"That's hard. That's harsh. I'm sorry for you. Still, I know how they think. You probably want to, you know, put your best foot forward. You don't have to lie. I'm not saying you should lie. I'm only saying, you know, like you don't have to tell them everything."

"So what should I write?"

"I'm going to have to give you a whole new set of papers. It's okay. Don't worry. I just thought that we were going to have you all signed up today. Then you would know by graduation that you were accepted. But it's okay. I'll do everything I can. But you are going to have to write this again different."

"Is it better if I write I want to be a doctor who flies planes?"

"Not here. Not on the application form. They want to know why you want to be a Marine."

"That is why. How am I ever gonna learn that elsewise? That's why I'm asking you if you — if the Marines — will help me learn the stuff I need to know." A bit of whining had crept into her voice and she took a deep breath, glad the waiter had placed the bowl of egg drop soup in front of her. "Chicken coming," he said to the Marine and turned away.

"Go ahead," said the Marine, "you don't want that to get cold."

The young woman bowed her head and blew across a spoonful of soup. She looked up at him. "Why did you sign up?"

"Who, me? I wanted to serve my country. And I wanted to be proud of myself."

"You weren't proud of yourself? Before?"

"What kind of question is that?"

"No, I didn't mean nothing by it. I'm just saying."

"Oh, I was plenty proud of myself. Believe it, girl."

"Did I say something bad? I'm sorry. I thought that maybe something happened to you. Like something bad. I'm sometimes not proud because I let people do bad stuff. To me. And I thought maybe, I don't know. Sometimes you can lose your pride and have to go and find it again. You know what I mean?"

"No, I don't think so. No."

"I'm sorry. Sometimes I just say some dumb-ass shit. I'm sorry."

"No no, don't worry."

"What did you write on the application?"

"I wrote that I wanted to serve my country. To defend freedom."

The waiter brought the moo goo gai pan, along with a metal pot of tea and two small cups. The Marine looked down at the food, then up at the young woman who was smiling at him. "What?"

"Nothing."

"No. Not nothing. What?"

"You just sound like one of those brochure things."

"You don't believe me? It's the truth. I can't help it I can't find no fancy way to say it. It's the truth."

"Well, it worked for you. You got accepted."

The Marine was chewing his food. He poured tea into both cups. "You know," he said, "maybe the Corps is not for you. Maybe you don't have to fill out a new application." He put down the teapot with a clang and heartily speared chicken and vegetables with his fork.

"Why're you getting all worked up?"

"Who says I'm getting worked up? The Corps just don't need nobody with a bad attitude, that's all." He quickly brought several forkfuls to his mouth and chewed.

"I meant it. I meant it. Don't take it like that. I don't have an attitude. It worked for you. You're in. That's good, right?"

The young man nodded, frowning.

"Here. You got something." And she reached across the table to brush a grain of rice off his tunic. He grabbed her wrist and she saw the fear in his eyes.

"I only wanted to brush the crumbs away," she said as he released her.

"I think we should keep this business," he said.

"Please don't be mad at me. You have to help me."

"You write whatever you want to write."

"Please. I didn't mean to insult you."

The Marine bent to his food and said nothing. The young woman spooned through the soup without eating. "Listen, I'm sorry. I just want to be accepted."

"Well, you got an A on the test and you only need to get a C so I think they will like to have you. But I'm not the one who has the say. You could be disqualified for lots of different things."

"That's the thing. How do I not get disqualified?"

"That's what I'm trying to tell you. If you keep it to like 'I love my country' or like about being proud to be in the Marine Corps, you'll be in because your test was good, real good. And I can put a word in for you, write a note that you got a good attitude and whatever and they should take you. They don't need to know you're living with your dying mother and all like that."

"I don't live with my mother. I live with my uncle. My mother lives in Atlanta. She's in the hospital there."

"Another reason why it's better not to write that on the application. Then you have to explain too much."

"It would be great to be able to tell my Moms that I got in. That would make her happy. If she knew before she passes that I'm going to be all right, that I'm going to be a doctor who flies planes, she could stop worrying so much about me."

"I guess that would bring her some peace then."

The young woman paused to consider the idea. "Yeah, peace is right. That's it. She'd have some peace."

She drank her tea, which was cold, and refilled her cup and his. "Can I ask you something?"

The young man gave a quick nod with a stern look on his face. The mood had changed.

"Are your parents alive?"

"They are. And I'm going to give you the quick version of the story and that's all: I don't talk to them anymore."

"Why not?"

"I told you. Quick version. Besides, this is business."

The Marine raised his hand to hail the waiter and gestured in a circle over his food to indicate he would take it with him. "Usually that's not what people ask me. When they ask me 'Can I ask you something?' Usually they ask me if they'll get sent into combat, you know, if they'll see action. Most of them join up because they want to."

The young woman shook her head. "Not me, oh no. I mean I would go, of course, if I got sent, but why would somebody want to?"

"A lot of people want to fight. Look at the world. A lot of people want to fight. Sometimes they ask me if I ever have any second thoughts about joining up."

"I didn't ask you either of those things."

"I know. That's good."

"Because I know you'd have to tell me what you think I want to hear."

"Girl, there you go again. Why you want to be like that now?"

"I'm just saying. I mean, it's your job to get me to join."

"I'm trying to help you to join."

"I know. I know. And I appreciate it. I already know I want to do it. This is the only chance I got to do what I want. But you know what I wish?"

"What?"

"I wish you would tell me that you understand because the Marines were your only chance, too. Because I see that. That's not hard to see. I'd just feel better if you told me, like, 'Me too.' "

"Whatever. That don't make much sense to me. We better go back to the office and get some new forms."

The waiter came with the check, a saucer of pineapple chunks with toothpicks, and two fortune cookies; he gathered up the dishes.

The Marine offered the cookies to the young woman, and after she had taken one, he cracked the other and opened the strip of paper.

"What does yours say?" the young woman asked him.

"I think this one is yours! It says, *Gather wise counsel, then delay no more.*"

"And you're the wise counsel, right?"

"You should listen to the rooster!" He held up his hands, his palms toward her, and smiled.

"Mine is *Nothing is sometimes the best thing to do.*"

"What's that supposed to mean?"

"I think it means that you should send the forms in that I gave you."

"But why? To see if I was right that they'll reject you?

"I want to know that this is right for me. If they don't think I could be a good Marine because of things that happened to me, then I believe them. And if you, the Marines, can't help me fly or be a doctor, I don't want to join 'cause those are the things I want to do."

The Marine leaned toward her across the table. "I tried to tell you how it works, that's all."

"So send my application in. Just like it is."

The waiter arrived with the check and a brown bag folded down and stapled at the top. The Marine sighed. "Okay," he said. "Okay." He took out his wallet. "I can't believe they don't have pupu platter," he said. "What kind of Chinese restaurant don't have pupu platter?"

"Here," she said, holding out some money. "This is for my soup."

"No no, the Corps pays for this. It's in my budget. It's on the Corps."

"No thanks, Corps." She shook the bills at him.

"I'm not taking that."

"Then leave it for a tip." She shrugged, put the money on the table, and began to slide from the booth.

"I don't get you, girl."

"That's right," she said. "I get that. I can see that."

SUNDOWN JESUS

My sister Colleen called late last Thursday and asked me to visit our Uncle Danny at the nursing home where Danny Jr. had to put him when he couldn't care for himself. The truth is that all the home health agencies refused to send their people to his house anymore, he abused them so badly. The men were all thieves who had come to take care of him only as a way to case the house for future burglaries that, of course, never took place. The women, he was absolutely certain, wanted him to make love to them, and all their protests to the contrary were merely evidence that, being young, they were not as perceptive about their erotic urges as he. After nine aides from four agencies, including one plain-clothes nun from Corpus Christi community outreach who lasted all of twenty minutes, Danny Jr. had run out of options.

So I went. Last week. It fell to me because there's just the three of us at this point out of the whole family: me, Colleen, and Danny Jr., and he's someplace in Afghanistan, looking for bin Laden I guess. Danny Jr. wanted to transfer power of attorney to me in the event that any medical decisions would have to be made, and I agreed that that made sense.

The first thing I saw when the receptionist buzzed me in was an old woman in a wheelchair bent almost double with her elbow on the armrest and her bony hand, ropy with blue veins, waving around above her head. She looked like somebody trying to make a shadow puppet of a swan. "Hello dear," she said.

"Hello. How are you?"

"Hello dear."

"Hello," I said again.

"Hello dear."

Music came from metal discs, perforated like showerheads, mounted in the ceiling at regular intervals so that the volume ebbed and swelled as I walked the long corridor — awful disco stuff, Donna Summer I think.

When I asked at the desk for Uncle Danny's room number, the nurse told me to wait and got on the phone. It was as if they were expecting me. "If you'll wait right here, sir, Dr. Diebenkorn would like to speak with you," she said as she hung up. "He's our medical director."

"Is something the matter with my uncle?"

She smiled or smirked, a little bit of both, and looked at me steadily. I felt a little embarrassed; she was right, it was a stupid question to ask in here. Of course something was the matter. Something was always the matter. You could smell that much, for godsake. Aides were pushing wheelchairs everywhere. The halls were full of slumped and sleeping white-haired people. A rhythmic shrieking punctuated Donna Summer pouring from the showerheads.

"I'm Dr. Diebenkorn, Lewis Diebenkorn," he said offering his hand. Clean-shaven, bow tie, bright smile, good grip.

I introduced myself.

"If you'd be so kind, I'd like a word about your uncle's condition." He put a hand on my forearm as if there were, or were going to be, a secret between us. "My office is just down the hall." He turned away and I was clearly expected to follow him. Maybe it was that, that imperious body language, but already, trailing him into his office, I didn't trust him.

"Sit down. Sit down."

I did so and took the envelope from Danny Jr. from my pocket.

"Your uncle is a difficult resident to care for. You probably realize that." He brought his hands together as if in prayer and rested his chin on his fingertips. "But I'm getting ahead of myself. Excuse me. How would you describe your relationship to your uncle? If you don't mind my asking. Would you say you're close?"

What was this about? "Yes. Well, we were close when my sister and I were little. I haven't seen him in a long time." I thought of the kitchen table at his house, the one with the shaky leg where we played endless rounds of card games and Monopoly, and Clue, which was always our favorite. We sat there after school or on Sunday after church, my uncle chain smoking, drinking a can of beer, using an empty for an ashtray, Colleen and Danny Jr. and I with our glasses of Tang, trying to determine if Professor Plum or Mrs. Peacock or Mr. Green was the murderer, with the rope or the gun or the candlestick, and where — in the billiard room or the conservatory or the ballroom. We learned to ask questions, to challenge the answers, to notice everything and arrive at the truth through a series of deductions.

"He hasn't had a visitor in quite some time," Diebenkorn said.

I explained that there were few of the family left and that Colleen was a single mom and Danny Jr. was overseas. I also let him know — I held up the envelope — that Danny Jr. had transferred power of attorney to me. I'd read it over and it was pretty straightforward: no heroic measures if his heart stopped, no life support, no autopsy. The autopsy part was especially important to Uncle Danny, who took great pride in the fact that he had never had surgery; he'd "never been cut," he would always tell us, as if that proved he'd taken good care of himself when, in fact, he'd abused his body nearly every way he could. I handed the envelope to Diebenkorn and while he examined the form, I looked around. The whole office was furnished in fake cherry from Staples. Along with his degree were various plaques that said Best this and #1 that. And of course a crucifix; it was a Catholic nursing home, after all. Not a crucifix as I remembered it from boyhood though, the plaster Christ with sunken eyes rolled up to heaven, blood dripping down his face, his beard, an open gash in his side, hanging heavy from the spikes in his palms; this Christ was robed and chasubled and floating half an inch in front of a plus sign, aluminum or pewter, bloodless and serene.

"Thank you for this," Diebenkorn said. "I feel more at liberty to talk with you now. You uncle has been refusing treatment and is, in my opinion as a physician, suffering needlessly. I'm sure you will see what I mean when you visit with him. We would like to start him on a medication for his depression."

"Depression."

"Yes."

"He's eighty-seven years old."

"That's neither here nor there, if you don't mind my saying so. We have three residents here at Mercy Manor who are ten years older than that. And quite healthy, I might add."

"I see," I said, although I didn't.

"We also expect that treatment would help with his sundowning as well." He went on to explain to me that many elders in "settings such as this" seem to lose their bearings as the day wears on, becoming disoriented and delirious, a form of pseudodementia that corrects itself by morning. "It can make the night a terrifying experience," he said.

One night, he told me, Uncle Danny had got it in his head that he was a prisoner of war, that he'd been caught behind enemy lines. He gave the aides a hell of a time, insisting he had to escape and rejoin his unit, calling them Nazi bastards, saying they'd get theirs when his unit arrived. Diebenkorn seemed to think this was amusing, or else he thought I would find it amusing. In either case, I refrained from telling him that my uncle had, in fact, been a Nazi prisoner during World War II. It was a subject he would never talk about, not a word. "We had to administer a sedative. Actually, we've had to do that several times. I have all his charts here showing the necessity of our medicating him, if you'd like to review them."

"I only came to visit him," I said. "I'd like to see him."

His desk computer dinged. E-mail. He glanced at the screen and turned back to me. "I'm going to ask you, as his power of attorney, to authorize us to treat his depression. I want to try an antidepressant first, and if that doesn't give him some relief, some ECT."

"And I can authorize this? Without his consent? Even though I haven't seen him for six or seven years?"

"You have power of attorney. And I can document that he is no longer competent to act in his own best interest."

"I want to visit with him."

"Of course you do." He pressed the intercom and summoned an aide, who arrived a few awkward moments later. "If I'm not here when you finish your visit, please have me paged. We'll need to talk again before you go."

The scene outside the office was chaotic and strange, a mix of lively staff and inert elders. My escort, Jorge, explained that it was Super Bowl Week and that the whole place was several days into a morale-building competition called the Care Bowl in which staff were awarded plus or minus points for different tasks: room cleanliness, resident grooming, and general cheerfulness were all subject to the awarding of points or demerits, and the staff members with the highest tally by the big game on Sunday would get a free dinner and a movie for two. We walked by a group of elders who were being urged to throw a foam rubber football into a wastebasket set up for the purpose. As we walked, Jorge let me know that Uncle Danny wasn't doing much to help his score, that he wouldn't even get out of bed. Jorge knocked on the door and announced, "Mr. Quinn, we have a visitor for you."

My uncle was propped in his bed and writhing in distress over a pillow behind him he couldn't reach. "Give me a hand here, willya? Take this one out. Take it out!" I extracted the pillow and managed to arrange the others to his satisfaction. I put the pillow on top of the plywood bookcase next to his bed. I remembered that bookcase from boyhood. His proudest possession, it was filled with The

Great Books. Every month another would arrive in the mail and take its proper place in the bookcase the publisher sent to each subscriber. On the wall above the bookcase was another hydroponic Christ drifting off his holy rood.

"So, Patrick, what brings you here?" I sat in the high-backed vinyl chair next to him. Even now, thinking back on that day, I'm moved by the look he gave me then. And don't dare bullshit me, it said.

"Came to see how you're doing," I said. His eyes narrowed, scanned mine. "How's Danny?"

"He's fine, I guess. He hasn't caught Osama yet." He kept his gaze on me and I read the fear behind it. "Uncle Danny, I wouldn't lie to you."

"Ha," he said. "Do me a favor. Raise me up with that thingamajig. Just a little."

Jorge knocked and asked if he could get us anything. "You can get the fuck out of here," said Uncle Danny. "I'm talking to my nephew. Georgy Porgy, that's what I call him. Christ, he's in here every five minutes trying to get me to go and finger-paint with the biddies in the rec room."

"He's trying to take care of you."

"Aw, you can't leave a fart in this place without somebody sniffing it and writing down what it smelled like. How's your sister? She get married yet?"

I told him that Colleen was happy. That her daughter Tanya had just turned three.

"I always figured her for a nun, you know. I remember how she used to carry all those holy cards in her little purse. You with your baseball cards and her with her saints."

I took the opportunity to steer the conversation to good memories. My good memories of him. I can't remember anyone in our family ever saying thank you or sorry, at least not to one another, but we certainly communicated gratitude or apology in other ways. Nothing was ever direct. I wanted to find a way to say thank you and sorry I hadn't been to see him in so long. I think he knew I was appreciative. The whole time I reminisced, he looked away. I tried to make him laugh with the story about the time Danny Jr. caught him cheating, sneaking a peek at the three cards in the envelope during a pee break while we were playing Clue. But he put his hand over his face as if I were freshly accusing him. "I see you've got all your books here. Catching up on your reading?"

He stared at the bookshelf. "I'm tired, Patrick. I'm all done. Everybody here is sick of me, including me. I'm sick of myself. I'm boring. I wake up every morning and say 'Aw, shit.' I'm ready to die. I don't have anybody else to say that to, and that's the truth."

"The doctor says you're depressed."

"That dipshit Diebenkorn? He wants me to take some of his happy pills. I told him right where he can tuck his pills. You can't know what it's like to be this tired. The priest here, what's his name — the Polish one — tells me to pray. And I do. Before I fall asleep I pray I don't wake up. Last week they took my belt, my shoelaces, even my hairbrush. Suicide watch. Like I was going to kill myself with a hairbrush. They had a nurses' aide in a chair by the door around the clock. Mostly she slept. One time I woke and saw her there so I clapped my hands and she jerked awake and looked at me. But just for a moment, mind you, then she fell back asleep. For Christ's sake, Patrick, I'm not going to kill myself. I just don't want to outlive myself."

I was struck, as I listened, with how frail he'd become. His gruffness had hidden his diminishment; maybe that was its function. Though he was still thick around the middle, his arms and legs were thin, shriveled, his wrinkled skin too big for them.

"You take these poor bastards here. Have you seen them?" He pointed to the door. "In pain, every goddamn thing there is to be wrong is wrong with them but they just can't die. Their hearts just keep banging away. You take a heart — I saw this on a TV show one time — you can take a heart out of a dead man's chest, suspend it in saltwater, give it a good electric shock and goddamn if it won't beat. A stupid muscle. Mechanical. I'm all done, Patrick. I'm just waiting for the wagon."

I leaned forward and touched him on the forearm. While I struggled to think of something to say — everything that occurred to me seemed wrong — he closed his eyes, heaved a loud sigh, and fell asleep. I watched his stubbled face for a while; a medley of muted emotions seemed to play on it until it slackened into a deep slumber.

Absent-minded and fidgety, I took Aristotle from the shelf. Stiff. Brand new. The spine uncracked. I put it back and took up Marcus Aurelius, which was just as unyielding. Virgil, Montaigne, Shakespeare, Pascal, Freud — not a single volume had ever been opened.

On my way back to Diebenkorn's office I had to cross an open space near the nurses' station where a dozen or fifteen wheelchairs were arranged in front of a screen, a slide projector behind them. Some of the old people had trays on their wheelchairs; others were kept from falling out by a sheet tied across their chests. A young woman, maybe twenty, an aide, was operating the projector, cracking her gum, asking cheerily as a third grade teacher, "Would anyone like to read this one?" Silence. Across the top of the screen it read, "THIS DAY IN HISTORY. January 26, 1945. The Liberation of Auschwitz." She cracked her gum again and read aloud: "The Libbershun of Aus, of Awsk, the Lie-ber-a-teeon of Askwits, the Liber. Liberation . . . " until an old man right in front of her, a long white cowlick rising from his head, rocking hard in his chair against the white sheet holding him, bellowed, "Auschwitz! Auschwitz!"

"Thank you! Boy, I had a lot of trouble with that one!" She changed the slide. "Who wants to read this one for us?"

I got slightly lost before I found my way back to Diebenkorn's office; the layout of the place was like a Parcheesi board, an open square in the middle, the nurses' station at the center of it, and four corridors radiating from there. I'd taken the wrong one and had to interrupt an aide who was in conversation with two others about the pool for Sunday's game.

"Have you had your visit?" asked Diebenkorn.

I remained standing. I guess I didn't want to stay any longer than I needed.

"We spoke. He's sleeping now."

"And? Do you see what I've been saying?"

"He wants to die," I said. "He says he's finished. He's tired."

"So you see what I mean. We're concerned for his quality of life."

"He has no quality of life. He doesn't want to be here."

"My point. If we treated his depression, he might come round to participating in some of our activities here. The staff tries very hard to match activities to residents' interests. But none of that is of any use if the resident is suffering from depression."

"Who do you like in the Super Bowl?" I asked him.

"Pardon me?"

"My uncle was a football fan all his life. Now he doesn't care enough to mention the game on Sunday."

"A deep depression can do that. The bottom line is that depression can be life threatening. And then there are his terrors, his sundowning. As I said, I think we can alleviate his suffering if you'll help us."

"No."

"I'm sorry?"

"No. I'm not authorizing any pills."

"No no, it's not just pills. The medication is only a part of the overall treatment plan."

"No."

"You could be saving your uncle's life. Let's give it a try at least."

I excused myself. Diebenkorn rose behind his desk but did not come around. He asked me to think it over and call him if I changed my mind.

In the hall, Jorge and another aide were trying to get a group of elders to play a game that involved keeping a pink balloon in the air. The ceiling speakers showered Sister Sledge on everyone.

Uncle Danny was still asleep, his jaw slack, tongue resting on his lower lip. I stood by the bed and stared at his momentary peace. The pillow was still on the bookcase. I could hear Jorge in the hall, "Tap it! Tap it! Up! Up! Aw. Okay, we'll try again!" The whole time I kept looking at Jesus adrift and off his cross.

As I left, the broken white-haired woman was still in her wheelchair by the door, her useless hand above her head. "Hello dear," she said.

"Hello." I smiled at her, and then I bent down close to her and whispered in her ear. "Colonel Mustard," I said, "with the pillow. In the library."

GUY LOOKS FOR WORK

Guy scanned the want ads. He was supposed to be looking for a job, of course, but as his eyes moved down the columns, the question of how to make some money quickly swelled into the panicked demand for the missing explanation for his life. Where did he fit? What was he supposed to do with a PhD in ethics?

He continued to scan the page. What the hell was an Assembler? What did an Assembler assemble? What did an Auditor listen to? An Estimator estimate? An Expediter expedite? And what in the name of God was an Oracle Developer?

Guy felt misunderstood. Well, not misunderstood, exactly, so much as not understood at all. As he went about his day, busy with first this and then that, so he went about his trackless life. On a good day he felt the equanimity of the disinterested spectator, bemused by the looks on peoples' faces, the intensity of their exertions, the occasional grace and justice of their actions. On bad days it was as if he were trapped in a meandering joke.

"Quit staring!" said Guy's wife.

Gazing into the middle distance, Guy was out of it again, as if he'd passed through a cognitive one-way door and couldn't get back in. His wife, Wanda, was at the table making a list on a special pad of paper with "TO DO" across the top and a vertical row of boxes inviting emphatic checkmarks. Guy understood that her list-making was a kind of prayer, an alignment of her intentions with her energy. One day he spent about half an hour looking at one of her checkmarks: it was, up close, a gorgeous bit of thoughtless grace. In the way it began, downward, hard, and then changed direction, gaining lift and velocity until it vanished, implying itself into the invisible, it was as perfect as any Zen master's brushwork O. Guy's heart swelled with love and appreciation.

"Oh, for Pete's sake," said Wanda when he tried to tell her, but he could see she was pleased. Wanda had half a dozen items on her list. She paused the slightest moment, never looking up from her paper, then wrote down half a dozen more to fill the sheet. "I'll be gone at least three hours," she said to Guy as she paused in the doorway. "You have any interviews today?"

Guy looked at her.

"Any prospects?"

"We'll see," he said.

Prospects, prospects. Anything was possible. Maybe a new species, the next evolutionary tsunami, was swelling in his consciousness even then; maybe there, in the middle distance, the utterly transforming notion of the next, the new, the unforeseen (though perfectly foreseeable in retrospect) Homo contemplatus *would come to birth among the dust motes glittering in the sun: the pollen, the cat dander, bird down, occasional mosquito, and airborne viral life, all charged with the same command to mutate toward perfection that had long ago inspired that first ancestral ape who, sucking on his fingers and scratching his ass, first glimpsed there, three or four feet from his nose, the irresistible idea of the human. Who could say?*

"Oh, for Pete's sake," Wanda finally said. She turned and harrumphed down the walk, her high heels clicking on the pavement.

Guy watched her behind and thought how lucky he was. He'd had the best education other peoples' money could buy, and he felt some responsibility to all the people who had contributed to his development as a thinker. That responsibility included the commitment to use his gifts responsibly, to "first, do no harm," and to exercise restraint. To Guy this clearly meant not doing anything at all when he was unsure what to do; not making things worse was, after all, as important as making them better. If he was patient, what he should do would come to him. He felt sure of that. He had determined a long time ago that no matter how many opinions there were about any course of action, no matter how many schools of thought, there was always another, not under discussion, that involved going back to bed.

He went back to bed.

HOW THE DEVIL GOT HIS HORNS

A jackass, his long ears lying back flat and his big teeth clack-ing with every word, was preaching a sermon to the assem-bled creatures. His post as preacher had been acquired by virtue of his loyalty to his master, whose cart he drew wherever he was told; in fact, his loyalty, much remarked upon, was really an abid-ing hunger for carrots, bunches of which were his for merely going where he was directed and pulling this or that load no questions asked.

He cleared his throat: *Ggrhawwwwwwww!*

A pig in the first row farted, loudly.

"Pew!" said the hyena behind him, shrieking with laughter. "Get it? Pew!" and he cracked himself up again, along with all the young nearby whose parents shushed them with stern looks.

"Today," said the jackass, "it is my sad duty to chastise you, my congregation, for your lasciviousness, your licentiousness, your concupiscence, and … and … and your scriptural, that is to say doctrinal, theological rebelliousness made manifest, shall we say, in the near catastrophic rise in the numbers of you who seem to believe that simply because spring has arrived you are free to frolic and to gambol, that is to say, to fornicate with abandon and at every opportunity!"

The rabbits bowed their heads self-consciously, wrinkling their noses, trying to muster some shame, some remorse, each of them becoming very quiet and inward-looking, listening for the still, small voice of self-correction, reform, and spiritual renewal, but all they could hear were their own horny little hearts thump-thumping in their soft delicious chests. To a one they resolved to look contrite until the service was over when they could head for the hedgerow lickety-split.

Not so the goat. He curled his lip and snorted; he stepped into the center aisle of the chapel and stomped the hard polished floor with a forehoof.

The jackass went on preaching. "Think on these things my brethren. Examine your conscience."

The pig let out a long, almost musical belch, echoed soon after by the mockingbird in the choir loft. The goat brought up some cud and chewed it, mulling the preacher's words.

"Ought there not to be in this world a race of creatures disciplined to restrain themselves, to submit to law and reason those bestial appetites that drive the merely pleasure-seeking weaklings among us? You know who you are, my brethren, stunted in your spiritual growth — you fornicators, lotus-eaters, profligates!"

The goat gulped back his cud and stomped the floor again. "You carrot-chomping, bucktoothed hypocrite!" he said. "You cannot, so you preach that we shall not. Your father was a horse, your mother a mule, and you are worse than a gelding, you bio-engineered hack! You cannot mate! You cannot reproduce! He begrudges us, dear friends, what he cannot have. I'll have no more of this garbage!" And with that, the goat clomped down the aisle and out the doors of the chapel.

This was news to the congregation and set them to mumbling and fumbling from the pews, filing out of the place and looking for places among the shrubs and tall grasses where they might take their private pleasures guiltlessly.

The jackass, from his pulpit, brayed and brayed to the empty pews.

When the jackass's master heard the story of that Sabbath morning, he did what all masters do — he thought about how to turn the situation to his own advantage. First he set about buying all the available carrots, lettuce, radishes, and what stores of nuts and apples had been laid by. Then he bought whatever property, especially tillable land, that he didn't own already.

Soon everyone was mighty hungry. Those few heads of lettuce that anyone might grow, those few hidden nuts wrapped in a rag in a drawer, became as precious as gold and nearly as expensive to buy. And of course with all that procreation going on, soon there were many more mouths to feed. The situation became desperate. Luckily, the jackass's master had been watching closely for the moment when his philanthropic impulses might be exercised to the greatest good and to his greatest advantage. The word went forward across the land that plenty of lettuce, radishes, seeds, apples, nuts, fruits, and hay were to be distributed after the services at the chapel each week, right after the sermon, and that all — pigs, cows, horses, sheep, all manner of birds, squirrels, and rabbits — were welcome. Everyone but the goat.

Little by little, those who meant never to set foot in the chapel ever again came back, bringing their hungry offspring. Soon, as the master had predicted, there was a whole new generation of devout creatures who listened, intent on not repeating the lecherous mistakes of their parents which, as they were told repeatedly, had brought about great misfortune.

Even the goat returned, but not in the flesh. No, he was represented everywhere, in story and painting, in song, in stained glass windows and pictures in prayer books: he became the tempter, the angel of darkness, the evil one. Even today you can see these representations of the archfiend with his goat's beard, cloven hooves, and horns.

As for the jackass, he is braying from the pulpit still. If you don't believe me, go and hear for yourself!

THE WRONG SUNDAY

Marty woke, sat up, and untangled the white rosary from the fingers of his left hand. His mother had given him the rosary for his nightmares. Now when he woke up frightened, he prayed to Our Lady to help him get back to sleep instead of waking his parents because his father needed his sleep to go to work at the truck plant in the morning. Mostly his nightmares were about things falling and crushing him. His mother said Our Lady would protect him, and his father told him that you can never dream you died because you always wake up right before.

He put the rosary on his night table, swiveled off his bed, and knelt to say his morning prayers. He looked up sideways at the plastic crucifix above his bed with the two brittle palm leaves thumbtacked below it and said an Our Father, a Hail Mary, and a Glory Be.

His father's shoes were outside his bedroom door as they were every Sunday, and Marty, still in his baseball pajamas, came downstairs to work on them. He could never get them to shine "bright enough to see your face in them," which was how his father said he wanted them, but it wasn't because he didn't try.

First, he spread newspaper on the floor as his father had shown him. "You don't want to get shoe polish on your mother's carpet," he'd said. Then he took an old sock, slipped two fingers into the toe, and used it to get out a good-sized wad of black polish from the flat can. He placed his other hand deep in his father's shoe and applied the greasy black polish thickly all over, taking special care to cover around the heel and along the sides of the sole. Then he put the shoe aside and did the other one. "You've got to let the goop dry on them a few minutes. That's the secret." After the other shoe was smeared with polish, Marty waited an extra couple of minutes before working on the first one, just to be sure. When he could wait no longer, he got down to the hard work. He balled up the sock and wiped off all the extra polish. Then he got up on one knee and put his foot in his father's shoe to keep it steady so he could work with both hands. The shoe was almost big enough for both his feet. He took another sock, a clean white one with a hole in the heel, and rubbed hard at first to work the polish in, then gradually more softly until he was lightly and swiftly drawing the sock back and forth over the shoe and around the back of the heel. Finally, he spit on it — all over, not just on the toe — and rubbed that in. Then the other shoe.

The shoes were old and had been resoled. On the left one there was a bump from his father's little toe and the leather was cracked there.

He had to give up again. Was it really possible to get them so shiny you could see your face in them? His father had told him that in the army, if the sergeant couldn't see his face in your boots, you had to clean the toilets for a month. Marty's mother always cleaned the toilet; she didn't seem to mind, but he didn't think he would like that job.

Not that his father ever complained. He always told Marty that he had done a good job, and he always handed him two nickels then, one for himself, and one for the collection basket at Mass.

Marty loved the smell of the shoes when he was through with them. He held them up to his face and rubbed the side of the heel against his cheek. Smooth. He put them at the bottom of the stairs and went back to place the socks and polish back in the shoebox and put it away in the closet; then he folded the newspapers and took them out back to the trash can.

He never got dressed for Mass until his mother told him it was time, so now he had a few minutes to himself. He could hear his father upstairs in the shower. He was singing:

Can she bake a cherry pie, Billy boy, Billy boy?
Can she bake a cherry pie, charming Billy?
She can bake a cherry pie
quick as a cat can wink its eye.
She's a young thing and cannot leave her mother.

Marty got his baseball glove from the back porch and practiced his windup in front of the full-length mirror in the hall. This was the second year his father had been coaching him. "Nah, cripes, you throw like a girl, Marty," he'd said. "Now watch. You throw from the shoulder, hard, and use your back, strongest muscles in your body in your back, that's where you get your power, and fol- low through, follow through!" So Marty leaned forward and made believe he was chewing tobacco and looked into the mirror for the catcher's sign. He nodded, spit to his right (although he only made believe, he would never spit on his mother's carpet) and went into his windup. "Rock back, rock back when you get your arms up," his father had said, "then shift your weight when you throw. You can feel it. Feel it? That's when you kick your leg out. Bring it over from the shoulder. Follow through, follow through!"

The phone rang, as Marty finished his windup and delivery, end- ing with his right hand almost touching his left knee, back bent but with his glove up in case the batter hit a line drive to the mound. He answered it on the third ring. It was his Aunt Elizabeth.

"I'm fine," said Marty to her question.

"Good. Now let me speak to your father, Sweetheart, okay?"

His father came down the stairs holding a towel around his mid- dle. He took the phone, and Marty went back to the hall mirror.

After a short time, his father hung up the phone. "Hey. Dad.

Watch!" said Marty, and he went into the stretch position his father had shown him and turned to his left to pick off the imaginary man at first base.

But Marty's father was standing naked, the towel on the floor, and Marty watched him slowly, very slowly, sit down on the floor and put his head down and cover his face with his hands.

Marty's mother had been coming down the stairs and now she went to his father and knelt beside him. She put her arms around him and he looked up. "My father is dead," he told her. Marty saw that something had happened to his face. It looked like it was melting like a candle. Marty's mother covered his father's lap with the towel.

Marty stood with his fist in his baseball glove and remembered that his father had a daddy too, and he thought about how he would feel if his daddy died. He thought about what he had just seen happen to his father's face, which was now hidden in his mother's hug. Was his daddy going to die too? What if God had decided to make today the day when everybody's daddy died? And then he understood, for the first time, that it was his grandfather who had died.

He threw down his baseball glove, ran upstairs to his room, and dove into his bed, crying now. He chewed on the corner of his pillowcase, and when he was quiet for a moment, he could hear his father moaning downstairs; then he stuffed his head under his pillow and cried again because it was a sound he could not stand to hear.

Soon he felt his mother's hand on his back, and she was saying something. He didn't move. His mother stroked his back and then began to pat his bottom. He withdrew his head from the wet dark under his pillow.

"You don't have to go to Mass today, Pumpkin, if you don't want to."

Marty stared at the crucifix. "I don't want Grandpa to be dead." He could feel his grandfather's scratchy face against his cheek, could smell his grandfather and taste the little swallow of beer he sometimes left in the bottom of the tall brown bottle, could see him lean from his great black chair and spit tobacco juice into the blue Maxwell House coffee can on the floor. He remembered his classmates laughing when he told Sister Eunice that his grandfather was the governor; that's what his father called him — "Howdy, Governor," he would say. His grandfather walked with two canes because something had fallen on his legs at the truck plant; Marty could see those canes right now hanging on the back of the black chair.

"I want to go to Mass," he said.

He walked the three blocks to the church alone, without crying, and arrived just as the previous Mass was getting over. People were coming out of the church and getting in cars parked on the baseball field next to the school. Marty went up the church steps, holding onto the black iron rail, against the crush of the colorful talkative faithful.

Inside, he could smell incense, and there were people still moving around in the choir loft, which meant that the Mass before had been a High Mass. Marty loved High Mass for the organ and the singing of the Kyrie and the Agnus Dei, but his father would never go because it took too long. He took a place in the third pew on the left, in the middle so no one would have to climb over him. He opened his missal to the prayers before Mass and looked at the picture there of an empty sanctuary with the trapezoid representing the arrangement of the starched pall covering the empty chalice and unconsecrated host in front of the tabernacle. He looked up at the altar, saw that it was so, and took heart. The Mass is the highest form of prayer, said Sister Eunice, and had been known to work miracles, even stop wars.

An altar boy came from the sacristy bearing a golden staff that ended in a small cone used to extinguish the candles. It was David Corcoran, the best pitcher on the school baseball team. Marty watched him put out the candles from the High Mass, one by one, leaving only the two that flanked the tabernacle. The smell of the curling smoke reached Marty, and he thought of the white roses in his backyard. Sister Eunice said that the altar candles were made only from pure beeswax, and Marty thought of the white roses not only because of the smell but because he liked to watch the fat, heavy, furry bees fumble over the roses and think that they were making the wax for the candles to worship Our Lord. He noticed that, under his cassock, David Corcoran was wearing worn gray high-top Converse sneakers.

Marty looked at the life-sized painted plaster crucifix above the altar. Jesus' body hung heavy and exhausted, blood running from his wounds, his eyes sunk in shadow, his loins draped with a cloth. He looked real except for a chalky spot where one toe had been chipped, and Marty tried hard not to look at that.

People filled the pew on either side of Marty. On his right was Mr. Lazzaro whose first name, Marty knew, was Gabriel, like the angel. He was said to be some kind of inventor, but Marty's father said he was a drunk who couldn't hold a job. An old woman with flabby, speckled arms knelt on Marty's left; leaning her rump on the seat, she was saying her purple glass rosary in a loud murmur.

The woman who knelt in front of Marty was wearing a stole made of three dead animals. Their snouts were flattened, and their paws hung detached from the surrounding fur. Marty could tell that their eyes were not real.

He wanted his grandfather back, but it was because of what had happened to his father's face that he wanted the miracle. He wanted his father's face, composed and serious, coaching him, showing him how to grip the ball across the seams. He wanted his father's voice, "Follow-through, follow through! Attaboy!" Not what he heard in his room and on the way out the door to Mass: his father's cries and moans, his mother comforting him.

A bell rang, and the priest and altar boys entered the sanctuary. Marty followed the words of the priest in his missal, the Latin the priest was saying on the left-hand page, the English on the right.

Et introibo ad altare Dei,	And I will go to the altar of God,
ad Deum qui laetificat	God who gives joy
juventutem meum.	to my youth.

The priest was Father Baxter who took over for Sister Eunice every Thursday morning to instruct the class in the catechism. Marty studied hard and tried to impress him because he was also the school baseball coach, and Marty's father had said that he'd be ready to go out for the team by the fifth grade. And even though that was two whole years away, Marty had set his sights on it already.

Marty had to move from the Ordinary to the Canon, in the back of the missal, to pray along with the priest who was saying the Introit in Latin, then back to the Ordinary with its pictures of all the priest was doing, then back to the Canon for the Epistle. He didn't want to be one of those Catholics Sister Eunice said merely attended Mass and didn't pray along with the priest. Soon everyone rose for the Gospel.

"From the Gospel of Luke," said Father Baxter, "Chapter 11, verses 33 through 36. And Jesus said to them: 'No man when he has lighted a candle, puts it in a secret place, neither under a bushel, but on a candlestick ....' "

Marty's face grew hot and his hands shook. The Gospel he had turned to was the wrong one. That meant that he had also read the wrong Introit and Epistle! He had turned the pages to the wrong Sunday. He'd been praying the wrong Mass.

Now there would be no miracle. His father's face as he had seen it when he sat on the floor, naked, holding his knees, would never disappear from his memory. The old woman on his left nudged Marty and said, "Shh," because he was grinding his teeth.

From the pulpit Father Baxter was saying, " ... and for the soul of our dear brother, Edgar Mueller, who died quietly in his sleep last night."

It was like retching, as if something was being pulled up out of him, out of his belly, and Marty made a loud sound that he himself didn't hear until Mr. Lazzaro put his arm around him and pulled him close. Marty flailed at him and broke away. The woman in the fur stole had turned around and was reaching toward Marty's eyes with a lace-bordered handkerchief but couldn't reach him. One of the animals' heads hung down, and Marty could see the sharp little teeth in its mouth. He stood up.

"He didn't wake up!" he shouted. "He didn't wake up!" And he scrambled to his left, walking on the padded kneeler, hand over hand along the back of the pew in front, climbing over knees and legs. In the side aisle he ran past three ushers standing against the wall holding the long-handled wicker collection baskets, past the dark mahogany confessionals, and into the vestibule where a round man with a red face, wearing a green plaid jacket, knelt down in front of the door and held out his arms to him.

"Hey, hey, take it easy, son," the man said.

Marty dodged and twisted and got by him and ran the three blocks home. When he arrived, his mother was at the kitchen table drinking coffee.

"Where's Daddy?"

"He went to Aunt Elizabeth's, Pumpkin."

"He's a liar!" said Marty. "He said bad dreams can never kill you, and Grandpa had a bad dream and he died!"

"Marty. Wait a minute. You don't know that for sure. Grandpa was very old."

His mother was holding both his hands. Although her voice had been gentle, Marty looked in her eyes and thought he saw that she was angry. "I'm sorry I called Daddy a liar," he said.

"It's all right, Pumpkin. You're confused."

He thought about what his father had told him and remembered the dream he'd had that night. He and his father were underneath the bleachers at a baseball game. They were looking for something in the weeds and mud. He could see the sunny field and the players through the legs of the people in the stands. There were paper cups and red-and-white popcorn boxes on the ground. "Look there," said Marty's father, "by your foot." It was a shiny nickel. Then the bleachers and all the people were falling down on them, very slowly and without any sound, and Marty heard himself shriek and woke sitting up in his bed.

"Suppose that Grandpa had a bad dream," Marty said to his mother. He thought of how long it took his grandfather to get out of his black chair and steady himself with his two canes. "Like something was going to fall on him? Something big? Then maybe Grandpa was too slow, because he was too old, or too tired, so that he couldn't wake up in time. Mom?"

"I don't know, Pumpkin. I suppose."

"But Daddy's not old," said Marty.

On Wednesday night Marty overheard his parents talking. "Absolutely not," his father said, "not after the display he put on at church on Sunday. He's to stay home from school and we'll ask Mrs. Mallon to come over for the day." Soon afterward his mother came upstairs to tell him.

Thursday morning, the day of his grandfather's funeral, he stayed in bed. The house was quiet. But he heard the tea kettle whistle and the clink of Mrs. Mallon's spoon on her cup in the kitchen. Earlier his father had come upstairs to talk to him. "You know what we're going to do next Sunday?" he'd said. "Next Sunday you and I are going to get up early, get in the car, and drive to Philadelphia for a doubleheader against the Cubs. How about that?"

His father had stood in the doorway in a black suit, white shirt, and black tie, wearing a brand-new pair of shoes.

GUY HAS A STORY TO TELL

But he doesn't dare tell it in the morning because nobody's ready for it; people are balancing paper cups of coffee between their knees while unwrapping their fast-food breakfasts, or they're rooting around in the cupboard looking for the pancake mix, or they're carefully measuring out spoonfuls of coffee while the water comes to a boil. Besides, if he told it in the morning, the dog would not want to go out, the cat would not want to come in, the rush-hour traffic on the bridges into the city would come to a halt, the little waves on the river would harden into something like frosting or stucco, birds would fall from the sky, and the nocturnal animals — raccoons, opossum, skunks — would stay awake to hear it. No way; he couldn't tell it in the morning.

Noontime seemed the perfect time, shadowless and relatively idle; but if Guy told the story then, the whole day would fall apart like two halves of a cantaloupe, the goopy seeds of everything that was going to happen ruined, exposed like film to the brilliant midday sun. Impossible. He couldn't bring himself to tell the story while the hour and minute hands, posed as if in prayer, pretended to be still, and he doubted anybody else could either.

Dusk is the time to tell a story, he thought. But then Guy noticed how for all the peace that seemed to accompany that delicious hour, it was plummeting into yesterday like an accelerating raindrop above a river and he couldn't bring himself to even begin. All the shops and businesses would remain open and the iron gates unlocked, people would sit immobilized on benches at bus-stops, chicks in their nests would grow desperate waiting for their parents, mice in the walls would crouch there in the first pangs of hunger, no bread would be cut, no plates passed across tables, no gossip about the day would transpire. Farmers coming in from the fields would stop with one foot in each of two plowed furrows, and the landscape outside the commuter train window would never change, nor the reflection of the faces equally available in the glass. On second thought, dusk would be a terrible time to tell the story.

It went without saying that he couldn't tell the story at night, partly because of certain episodes in the story itself, not to mention its themes, but also because walking around the whole day carrying a story you can't tell is wearying to the point of exhaustion, and Guy needed to sleep. Besides, it was a dark story, and at night the dark is too complete to augment with further darkness. The story would disappear, a shadow into shadow, ink into an inkwell, a panther deep into the jungle, a Black Maria idling, headlights off and far from any streetlamp. Unthinkable to tell the story at night. Out of the question.

Guy can only even try to tell the story if he starts in the split-second before first light, the moment before the roosters notice and kickstart the day, drowning him out with their habitual jubilation, along with the last bitter hissing cat brawl of the night, church bells, engines starting, barking dogs, and the first alarm clocks. It's the best Guy can do: "Once," he manages to say at that exact right moment, but then another day, with neither memory nor forethought, with its trillion stories, breaks.

FROM THIS DISTANCE, AT THIS SPEED

Early morning. Beside the interstate, westbound, on the way to my father's house, two men stand on a wooden scaffold before a blank billboard. The billboard is new: the bottom a green enamel trellis, the sign space perfect white, not painted over, and with two flood lamps on long pipes that hook over the top. One of the men is quite fat so that the other appears to be tall and very thin. A motorist at this early hour, passing a mile a minute, might be put in mind of Laurel and Hardy. Then acres again of young corn. It is June.

The heavy man, the elder, wears a V-neck white T-shirt and soiled plaid pants. The T-shirt rides up, and nowhere do his shirt and trousers meet. When he bends to pick up a chart, the cleavage of his substantial rump is visible. He smokes a cigar and from time to time white ash falls and remains on the sill of his ponderous belly until he brushes it off. Now he blows smoke at the chart in his hand, tips back his Braves baseball cap, and slowly shakes his head.

Okay, we'll call him Ollie.

Therefore it is Stan who is now on one knee, stirring paint and staring at the multi-layered spatterings of who-knows-how-many previous jobs, the boards of the scaffold itself more beautiful than any sign he can remember. He would like to paint one billboard like this, no lines, no shapes, no words: colors, numberless rosettes of color upon color, suggesting depth, approaching without the facile trick of perspective the truly three-dimensional; a profusion of color that beckons to be entered, the illusion of infinite joy.

No matter what Stan's story is, it must be as grave and unjust, as fearfully aware of its own unwanted end, as anyone's; therefore, because it is morning and he is there, wearing bleached white overalls and a paper cap, he must be thinking this, regardless of what else is on his mind, as he stirs the paint and loses himself to the past's alluring opalescence.

Ollie is different. He has disguised himself in fat, preferring to suggest that he is unacquainted with the fabulous. Behind his chart, behind his smoke, behind his flesh, what he is thinking would be obvious even to the passing motorists if they were not struggling to awaken or rehearsing conversations in their heads at 60 mph. Ollie's thought springs lightly, full of grace, freer than Stan's because he keeps it well-protected. He has a vision. Like Stan's, it is made of remembered and longed-for paint. Ollie believes in a painting in which every line is true. He has had more years to watch the scaffold thicken with chromatic history, and it doesn't gladden him as it once did. Let Stan believe there's something to be learned from beauty that merely happens by itself. That's what a young man is supposed to think. Old men know better, or at least know different, and are monstrous when they don't.

Ollie flicks a broken cylinder of white ash from his belly too late again, another hole burnt in his T-shirt, the price of concentration. The chart in his hand is the billboard in miniature, to scale, and colorless. The colors are named: Blue 3-1, Red 6-1-2, Yellow 2-1-4, etc. He knows what all these numbers mean, but the mixing is Stan's department.

Stan is a young man passing a familiar way, so Stan is, in a way, his son. There are just two of them, and it is early in the day. Okay then, Stan is Ollie's son.

Now it is just the beginning of morning rush hour. A trooper stations his car across the highway behind a billboard. "LET THE SUN SHINE," it says. "WNOW," it says. Stan and Ollie painted it a short time ago. The sun is a smudge through dark gray clouds. As the traffic increases, a helicopter clatters overhead. More people paying no attention pass. Each car says *wish*.

Stan has always liked to paint, but the assignments neither please nor challenge him. There is no green like this young corn in the sun, no blue like the distant mountains, no paint the color of his flesh. Though no one notices, he modifies the prescribed colors, heightening or deepening so that he must take extra care to keep his color scheme harmonious throughout; it is the only way he can maintain his interest. Ollie he cannot understand and wishes he sometimes had another partner, someone less trouble, lighter, not his father.

The background color, a shade of yellow, is ready.

Ollie hums to himself as he blocks the space, enlarging the sketch on the chart and writing in the numbers for Stan. For Ollie this is a fallback career, not what he wanted at all. He wanted to paint white lines. Growing up, he had wanted to be one of those unselfish, unacknowledged legislators, and he practiced day and night so that not a wave, not a ripple, not a wiggle ever marred the sureness of his beautiful boundaries. He painted parking lots and football fields, tennis courts and polo grounds, but he was never assigned a highway, not even a two-lane road. Those were the men whom he respected most—entrusted with people's lives,they were an elite corps, champions of humanitarian accuracy. The examiners, however, had found him insufficiently concerned with where the roads were going, and it was true that he could not have told you where a single road originated, what it passed, or where it ended. What made Ollie bitter, what seemed most unfair, was that no one had ever told him he needed to know that, and although his greatest pleasure had been to lay down the razor-edged lines of a parking plaza or the boxes within boxes of a tennis court, his pride demanded he resign. So for twenty-five years he has been painting billboards.

Stan is worried. Stirring an extra splash of white into Green 11-

7-2 with a narrow wooden paddle, he sees no future for himself in this. More and more billboards, owned by advertising firms, are given over to the lithographed campaigns of cigarette and soft-drink companies. Guy dunks a broom in paste and slaps it up there, three rolls for a twelve-footer, four for a sixteen. Done. A quarter of an hour for a cowboy and his cigarette, a co-ed and her cola. His father says that there will always be a market for the best and puts his hand, holding both a chart and an acrid dead cigar, on his shoulder. Stan knows it's hopeless, but it's Ollie's dream and Ollie is his father and he loves him. In other words, he has come to feel that if he doesn't make the same mistakes his father made, he's guilty of betrayal. When Stan is angry he decides his father makes him feel this way deliberately, or at least halfway so, intending to make him feel guilty but convincing himself he is trying to be encouraging. At other times he knows full well his father is only Ollie, fat and aging, doing the best he can, and Stan feels better then, more patient with the few years they have left upon the scaffolding together, executing one sign or another, following instructions.

Traffic begins to thin to midmorning numbers. The trooper leaves his post across the highway, tires crunching gravel, a cloud of dust and exhaust blowing north. The wind is up, flapping Ollie's trousers and blowing Stan's paper cap far off into the matchless green and regular rows of corn.

No different from other people, these two have to be imagined or ignored. What are their aims, their shames, their hopes? Where, among the possible relations of fathers and sons, is the truth of their connection? A traveler, from this distance, at this speed, is allowed, encouraged, perhaps enjoined by charity to consider them and speculate. They are, after all, on a kind of stage:

OLLIE:

These few precepts in thy memory look
Thou character (they are not from a book

But from my life are most hard wrung
As from a handkerchief of tears). Along
Your voyage may they stead thee well
For they are all is given me to tell:
Eschew false choices, ever find the third
Thing left withheld, occult, unoffered.
Judge not other persons by your wants;
They may have had the same dreams once
But changed them, tempered by necessity.
Neither a worrier nor a pretender be
For worrying oft fogs the view of port
And a pretender is an empty craft. In short,
Give what thou hast; take only when in need;
Strive to be genuine in thought and deed.

STAN:

Most humbly do I thank thee, good my lord.
Was e'er a son so well provided? One word
Of thy loving admonitions for estate
Would leave me boundless rich; oh happy fate
To have this tender hand upon my shoulder!
Inspirited am I, assured, made bolder.

The morning is ideal and the work goes well. By noon, much of
the background is finished, delineating half an open Bible and half
a message in hollow, stenciled letters. The traffic swells again and
moves a little faster. The trooper returns to his post.

Stan and Ollie change places so that Stan can begin, after lunch,
to flesh out Ollie's sketched enlargement of the right side of the
chart. They pass each other carefully, the scaffold narrow and pre-
carious.

Stan pours hot water from his thermos into a Styrofoam cup of
oriental noodles. The rest of his lunch is an apple. When he fin-

ishes, the empty cup gets away from him; he hates litter and tries to follow it so he can retrieve it later. In the wind, the cup seems to move like a small animal, scurrying from stalk to stalk, stopping, darting, finally disappearing. Stan imagines it coming to rest right next to his paper cap.

Ollie opens his black lunch pail and takes out two sandwiches he wrapped in foil the night before. He hesitates a moment to play a game with himself: one of the sandwiches is ham and Swiss, the other olive loaf and white American—he asks himself which one he would prefer to eat first and decides on the olive loaf; then he tries to guess which one is which. He opens the ham and Swiss. He will have to eat it first—rules of the game.

"Story of my life," he says to himself. He folds down the wire retainer that holds a 16-ounce can of beer in the lid of his lunch pail—warm, but it can't be helped—and expertly lifts the tab to open: *fit*, it says. Between sandwiches he will eat a bag of pretzels. For dessert, a cinnamon bun.

Ollie insists on taking the full hour for lunch. Stan is annoyed; he can remember several jobs they could have finished earlier.

Okay; but if Stan and Ollie are no different from sons and fathers elsewhere, they have quarrels rooted in frustrations more important. The love between sons and fathers must continually be renegotiated.

Stan is working to suggest the silken sheen on a purple ribbon laying across what are meant to be columns of text but are not meant to be legible. He sees Ollie finish his lunch, glance at his watch, and settle back to nurse the last few swallows of his beer. He trespasses on his father's peace.

"It's not as if you need me, Dad," he says. He has rehearsed a hundred ways to begin this conversation, and now he believes he is jumping right in; in fact, he is appealing to his father's fear and pride at the same time to throw him off guard.

Stan should know better. By now he ought to understand that his father's love is sentimental: he is capable of astounding gentleness, but only when things are simple. Ollie interprets emotional confusion as the result of an attack and counters at once with invective.

"It's not as if you neeeeed me, Dad," Ollie whines. "You little pissant! Need you? Only thing I need you for is to balance the friggin' scaffold."

Stan, despite his umbrage at being mocked, cannot stanch the chuckle rising at the notion that his hundred forty pounds offsets his father's jumbo counterpoise.

"You always were a quitter," Ollie barks from around the cigar in his teeth. "I'm tryin' to see you set up nice, line up your ducks. Then I'm out of your way. You think I couldn't leave tomorrow? Today? Right now? That's what I said—right now—you heard me right." He has got himself up on one knee and is pushing hard with both hands on his thigh to stand. The scaffold sways, and Stan's brush whacks a purple splotch on the empty Bible's binding.

"Just once!" Stan shouts. "Just once I'd like to talk to you without you blowing up and mocking me and giving me that martyr stuff. Look what you made me do." And then he mutters, not sure in his anger if he means for his father to hear, "Fat old stupid fool." Trying to remove the purple stain, he knows he has the momentum to keep on going, to shout now that there are no ducks ... face facts ... a life of his own ... the shrinking future ... the endless possibilities of color ... but he looks at Ollie.

Ollie's leaning forward, fists on hips, legs spread, face red, but Stan sees his eyes for an instant, wet and stricken, spiritless, before his father once again impersonates his simple-hearted self. He heard.

Though Ollie tears his cigar from his mouth and flings it away; though he bellows curses at his son and sneers and shakes his fist; though he says, "Go 'head and quit, you smart-ass. I got other fish to fry too, hot shot. Arizona! Arizona's where I'd be right now if it weren't for you"; though an ugliness that looks a lot like hate distorts his features, Stan is sorry. He believes he never meant to hurt his father. He tells himself he doesn't really think his father is stupid, or a fool; he feels that he has somehow cheated, the way his father has always cheated, by stooping to abuse.

Ollie has always wanted Stan to venerate him, to extol his virtues in anecdotes beginning, "Once my father…" or, "My father used to say…"; he believes, so deeply that he doesn't know it, that a father, any father, is a saint, a tyrant, or a fool. To be called a "fat old stupid fool" by his son is a kind of mortal wound: both saints and tyrants are remembered, fools are not. What's more, he wasn't meant to hear it, or so he believes, which means to him that this is what he comes to, finally, in the eyes of his son. Ollie can feel himself bleeding: dreams, pride, purpose, hope.

"You little scum!" he screams, and his voice squeaks. "I give you everything I have and it isn't good enough for you, eh, hotshot? Fine. We finish this friggin' holy-roller sign I'm out o' here and I don't give a Flying Wallenda's jockstrap what you do!"

Stan wants to say "I'm sorry, Dad," but that's what he says when he rocks the scaffold. He is aware of what his words have done and his transgression looms, bloated, like the incomplete, illegible Bible he's been trying to make appear three-dimensional. He has never called Ollie "Father," and for a moment he hopes that by saying something like, "Forgive me, Father, I was wrong," the words might resonate enough to assuage his father's pain, but he knows it would be lost on Ollie. He has never called his father anything but "Dad," so "I'm sorry, Ollie," is impossible and insulting. Because he has cried for Ollie before, in secret, often, and then resigned himself to patronizing him; because he has tried to canonize him, as Ollie wants, to make things simpler; because he has sworn to leave a hundred times and has not been able to, he says "I'm sorry."

"Sorry? Not as sorry as you're gonna be. You think I'm kiddin'."

"No. I know I hurt you, Dad. Father. Ollie. I didn't mean to. I'm sorry."

"Argh, you're a waste o' good sperm. Hand me that brush. Forget it. It was nothing, the weather, the worries, those damn Chink noodles you insist on eating."

While they work in silence, layers of smoky clouds shift, allowing the sun to brighten now this green patch of corn, now that; nevertheless, a sparse rain falls, the fat drops splatting like accelerated snowflakes on the billboard and scaffold. A big drop splashes on Ollie's nose.

"Sun shower," he says, "look for a rainbow." Stan wipes his brush on the fluted rim of the paint can and looks; since he's been old enough to understand he's heard this every summer, every time it rains, "Sun shower — look for a rainbow." Together they attend to the horizon, but there is no rainbow this time.

The evening rush hour begins. Traffic moves even faster than in the morning; people are speeding home to relax. The trooper pulls onto the interstate, his blue lights flashing, heading east.

Stan and Ollie work slowly; although the days are getting longer and the sky has cleared, neither wants to finish the job today.

"The light's no good from this angle," says Stan, "can't get the colors right."

Ollie wonders what the light has got to do with it; the colors are predetermined, coded, fixed, but he's afraid to ask. Stan's awful touchy these days. Besides, it'll take awhile to seal the cans, clean the brushes, pack up the gear. Ollie doesn't have another sign, another job, lined up yet. "May as well knock off," he says.

"Soon as I get this letter done," says Stan. He is working on the message now, what he and Ollie call the "pitch." A gnat finds the light in his eye. "Damn bugs," he says, blinking and rubbing his eye with his wrist.

"Gnats," says Ollie, watching their extemporary reel, "good day tomorrow. Sunny."

> *When gnats come out to dance and play,*
> *The next will be a sunny day,*

recites Stan to himself—another of his father's predictable small wisdoms. Near tears, stanching them by flaring his nostrils and breathing rapidly, he wonders how to efface that moment when he saw, in his father's eyes, that naked plea for mercy. Gnats dive at his shining eyes. There is nothing worse, he thinks, than to see one's father as—no, not a fool, not a fool exactly—as a sort of sad clown, beaten, lovable, but with only a sentimental, selfish, indulgent love, to see him as an old vaudevillian parroting the same one-liners every day. A Flying Wallenda's jockstrap? The quasi-wicked snigger of a waste o' good sperm? Can I unsee what I saw today? Unthink my thought, ununderstand? Will time splash other colors over this, restain it, paint it out? He wonders, sadly. "Look for a rainbow. Sunny day tomorrow."

Stan puts the finishing serif on the letter *N*. He has changed the typeface called for by their customer, Hope Second Reformed, because he feels more comfortable with the Old Style Roman than with Gothic. "IT IS WRITTEN" it will say until tomorrow.

Ollie's hungry. "Gotta take care of the corporation," he says, slapping his belly. By now, the sky to the west is tinged with coral and a cool translucent orange. For Ollie, sundown is a demarcation, and his dinner is a sacrament whose object is renewal; his heavy dinner starts the ritual release from consciousness of all that happened since the morning, a vespers of fullness and forgetfulness, an evening of relinquished worries and sleepy peace. For Ollie this is wisdom—to emerge from the day like a dog from a ditch and shake it off. "Shake it off," he's always told his son when Stan was hurt. Hit your thumb with a hammer? Disappointed? Frightened? Grieving? Shake it off, man, shake it off. Though he professes no religion, Ollie is a man of faith. Tomorrow will be new.

Carefully, hand over hand on the heavy ropes, rhythmically, habitually compensating for each other, balancing, they lower themselves and the scaffold to the ground. Ollie places the paint cans, soaking brushes, rags, plumb line, and chalk beneath a tarp at the foot of the billboard. The mercury lamps, on photo sensors, come on silently and flatten and distort the colors and perspective of the uncompleted sign with lunar light. Stan looks down the waist-high rows of young corn, thinking, for a moment, of his cap; when he turns, the regular rows disappear and he faces a solid green that looks dusty and blue and dull in the vaporous light. He is afraid. Tonight he will look at all his heavy lap-sized books of reproductions, hoping to find his aspirations still alive, and he knows already that he will not sleep.

In their battered pickup, Ollie driving, they bounce along the unpaved road to the nearest ramp and pull onto the highway eastbound. It is almost dark and there is hardly any traffic now. Most people are home, finishing their evening meal. Many will read, or watch television, or nap. Some few will begin to do what they have wanted to do all day. One or two, in a troubled solitude, will step outside to look at the sky, naming to themselves those few constellations they recognize.

ARE YOU WITH ME?

Weeks before the event, posters began to appear in town, each day more of them — on lampposts, on trees, in shop windows — until you could not escape knowing that the great and illustrious artist Pomo Pursnipov was coming to town to perform. Besides the date and time, and the place — the village green — the posters quoted several important sounding journals citing Pursnipov's literary genius.

"Here are stories with the potential to lift and inspire," wrote one critic.

"Nothing short of enlightening," opined another. "Will set your heart pounding and your mind aflame."

"Let Pomo Pursnipov set you on the righteous path to regaining what is rightfully yours."

By the day of the event, there were hardly any in the town who declined to attend. The green was crowded with people. The evening's maestro, the celebrated Pursnipov, led by an escort in a gendarme's cape with a lion's head clasp and a backwards Yankees baseball cap, walked through the parting crowd from the rear and ascended the three steps to the band shell. All eyes were on him as he sipped from a glass of water and surveyed his audience. Then he ducked down behind the podium, out of view for a moment, and replaced his water glass. Straightening, he cleared his throat and began:

"I came here to tell you a story." Here he paused. "However, I shall tell you neither of the stories you want to hear. The two you want to hear you want to hear in order to be assured that things are working out. They're not, in case you didn't notice.

"In the first story — which is true, by the way, so far as it goes — a peasant, a worker, a pauper, perhaps represented by a ragged barnyard fowl, in any case some animate emblem of the dispossessed, lives at the foot of a mountain. On the top of this mountain is a castle filled with all the riches of the earth, enough to buy and sell our hero's destiny a million times over. Are you with me? Does this sound familiar? Of course it does.

"The rest of the story is a string of predictable station stops that if I were to tell it, I would carefully disguise by adding detail. In your case, seeing as this is a city with cosmopolitan aspirations — like our hero, but more on that later — I would fashion episodes in which our hero — or heroine — happens upon a benefactor or finds a magic something—lamp or lotto ticket, it hardly matters—or wins a scholarship, but!" And here he raised his hand for emphasis. "But he proves, by way of several complementary episodes, that on his way up the mountain he has not, emphatically not, lost the common touch. Call him — where am I? — okay, call him something that impedes his progress up the mountain to the castle — you tell me .... Come on now, don't be shy." And here the artist cupped his ear and beckoned with his other hand. "What's that? I'm sorry, I can hardly hear you. What? Manuel!"

People looked around at one another and behind them; no one had heard anyone say anything.

"Manuel! Yes, that's good! You're good at this! Man well. Hispanic. Also a hint of "manual," by hand, a laborer, Manny, macho, and so forth. Great! Already in the file of stereotypes. No no, don't be offended, I'll be sure to describe his features so fully even you won't notice that at his core he's a cartoon.

"At least that's what I would do if I were going to tell you that story. But, come on, you have heard it before. You know it by heart.

And every time you sit there and listen to some variation of it, you make a terrible mistake. You listen and once again identify with the exceptional underdog. Your children watch you, want you to be proud, and they begin to dream of the climb. That's what I've been trying to demonstrate here.

"So … what are the trials we'll put our hero through on his way to occupancy of the castle? I promise you that any of you can do this if you let yourself. What trials? Anyone? Come on, you've heard the tale a thousand times." And here, once again, Pursnipov cupped his ear and leaned out over the podium. "Yes? What's that? A jealous rival? A wicked uncle? A wound? Yes, good, good, good. You see? Now there's a story you can sell!"

The people were once again looking around to see who had responded to the artist's question, but Pursnipov was going right on, so they quickly turned their attention back to the stage. "Throw in a complication at the end, in the final hour, and never, ever, question whether the company of those who live on the mountaintop, whose castle draws our hero like a magnet, are worth the trip.

"Not that it would matter if you did — that's just another way of telling the story. Gives it legs. You can throw in that alternate ending from time to time, but not too often. I mean, you can say at the end that it isn't worth the struggle and that the people at the top are vile, but the story's already done its work. Adrenaline has flowed. The ear has heard the music. The imagination is engaged. Sure as a certain rhythm gets your toe to tapping, you've been seduced again by god and now you'll listen even more attentively the next time, wondering which twist comes at the end. You're trapped. But maybe not so easily from now on. Maybe you'll hold out for a new story, a better one. If so, I shall be gratified, and proud if I have helped you see a way out of the usual darkness."

He disappeared from view for a moment, stood drinking a glass of water, disappeared to replace the glass under the podium, then stood looking at them for a long moment before he continued.

"So, that's the first story. Call it the dominant story. So I guess we can call this the recessive story. Yes, like genes on a strand. Like DNA. I can tell by the looks on some of your faces you already know what I'm going to say. I know you don't want to hear this, but bear with me. That only goes to prove my point, don't you think?

"The other story I won't tell, that you want me to tell, that you think that you need me to tell, is the one where—call it the Samson story—call it the Robin Hood story—the one in which our hero Manuel—here we might call him Emmanuel—redeemer, savior, one who comes to set things right, redress all wrongs, reset the switches, and establish harmony on the far side of justice, in short, to give the castle dwellers their comeuppance—does his famous stuff. He brings the house down, to turn a phrase, because he has never forgotten his roots, and because he refuses to participate in the oppression and exploitation he cannot manage to keep from seeing, hard as he tries.

"There's a good opportunity for a back story here, about lovers parted and rejoined."

Suddenly, he leaned far out over the podium with his hand to his ear again.

"What's that? What's that? That's right! I see you're getting in the spirit of this!" He pointed somewhere midway and to the left in the crowd, but no one was ever sure who he had pointed to. "Did you hear what she said? She said the hero, Emmanuel, has a girl-friend! That's right, a girlfriend from the old neighborhood who reminds him of the world he comes from. The memory, or maybe the possibility, of her love pushes him to a crisis of conscience. But now it's not a question of returning, of turning away from the life at the castle. It's a fierce moral struggle now! He sees the enslavement of his own people and his rage at this injustice brings him to turn against the castle dwellers.

"Maybe you double up the lovey-dovey stuff by giving him another girlfriend at the castle, someone he has fallen for on his way up the mountain, someone he has to spare when it all blows up.

"Be honest. Do you really want to hear that one again?"

All was quiet.

"Oh shit. You do. Of course. I told you to be honest and you were.

"But the stories we need are different from the stories we want. Maybe Manny is a storyteller now. Not to be self-serving, but maybe that's what it means to be a hero these days. Maybe all he can do is try out stories that make us less fearful, stories that change what we want. Maybe Manny is Manuela. Maybe Manuela is a kind of Cassandra. Maybe she tells the stories she does in the hopes that no one will have to live them. Maybe that's why she tells you what you don't want to hear. Maybe she is Maria, from Mare, the sea, Mnemosyne, the salty memory, the mother of the muses, life-giving, moon-dancing bath of beginning.

"Never underestimate how shrewd a storyteller she is. No matter where she might take you, her every story begins the same way: 'Once upon a time, a child was born.'"

Here the maestro ducked and retrieved his water glass. All eyes were upon him as he drank deeply. Then he ducked down as if to replace the glass, but this time he never stood up again. The people waited, confused, until a man in the first row, deeply concerned for the artist, hopped up on stage to find no one there at all.

"He's over there!" someone shouted as Pursnipov climbed into the car driven by his caped escort. The car sped off only moments ahead of the first cries from the men discovering their wallets gone, and the women with their empty purses.

GUY GOES UP TO THE PEARLY GATES

He looks around for a fancy ironwork gate set in maybe pink marble among billowing clouds — he knows it's idiotic, but he can't help himself; it's not that he expected it to be that way, really, but what soon comes into focus is hard to believe: three men in uniforms, one behind a desk and two on either side of what looks for all the world like a metal detector. They're all three in blue pants, white shirts, wearing peaked caps with shiny black bills. The one at the desk with the epaulets and the gold braid on his cap is him: PETER, it says on the brass identification bar over his left breast pocket.

"You ready?" says St. Peter.

"Pardon me?"

"Perhaps," says St. Peter. He begins turning the pages of a book as big as the one that Guy's Uncle Louie used to lug around of his wallpaper samples when he was in the decorating business.

"We see it all from here, of course. A guy like you," St. Peter says, "Come on, tell the truth, a guy like you, a guy like you named Guy" — and here he looks right and left at the other two and rolls his eyes — "he's sort of a man's man. Would you say that about yourself? That you're kind of a guy guy, Guy?"

Guy tries to shrug, but nothing happens. The saint laughs. "We see that all the time. Don't be offended, I'm not laughing at you. It's just that here we can't do that, shrug. It's endearing, actually, but here we deal in consequence, so shrugging is out of the question. Says here you have two children. Boys."

"Yes. Yes sir. They're fine boys. Were. Are. I'm sorry, I'm confused."

"And what did you teach them?"

"Teach?"

"The boys. Your boys."

"I taught them teamwork. Loyalty. Leadership."

"I see."

"That's good, isn't it? Right? That's good."

"Depends on the work, the object, and the need, respectively."

"So was I wrong then? I mean, I don't really get what's going on here."

"Good! I see you've come with your desire to understand intact. That's good. But you're reading this all wrong. You'll see. This is more burlesque than parable. By the time you get here, you're out of time, so parables are useless. Step over here, please."

Guy is facing a security checkpoint: a gate. "Please step through the pearly gate, sir," says one of the others, presumably an angel, in a white shirt and starched black trousers. Guy notes that the gate is indeed pearly, but not made of pearl. It has the pearly purple sheen of a knob of bone. He passes through and the alarm, a cross between birdsong and windchimes, sounds.

One of Peter's helpers comes forward with a security wand. He starts removing the offending articles. "What have we here?" the angel says, and with a flourish he seems to whip Guy's lungs right out of his chest. They're blue and red, and as he holds them up, they appear to be a pair of boxer shorts. He gives them one good shake, flaps them so they make a loud noise, thwapping like a snapped towel. He brings them to his nose and sniffs.

"Cut that out," says St. Peter, "that's disgusting."

"These are fine, a little smoky," the angel says as he throws them over his shoulder. They catch on the elbow of his wing, which Guy now notices for the first time.

"Military service?" says St. Peter.

"No."

"No?"

"Is that a bad thing?"

"Could be. It depends."

"On what?"

The angel and St. Peter exchange what look to Guy like worried glances. St. Peter makes a note. "Better pat him down," he sighs, shaking his bald head. "You're not supposed to ask that, Guy."

"Why not?"

"Because you're supposed to know," says the angel. "Uh-oh. What's this?" He has taken the item from Guy swiftly and soundlessly the way a magician might take a coin or an egg from behind a child's ear. He holds it up for inspection. It looks like a squid and Guy sees it is his heart.

"Gimme that," says the other angel. The heart's squidlike appendages are wriggling.

"No you don't. It's mine," says the angel with the wand.

"Oh come on, just a taste. At least save me one of the tentacles."

"Will you two cut it out?" says St. Peter. "Just give me the information. How many tentacles?"

"Eight," says the angel with the wand. "No, nine. Sorry. And there may be a little one growing here on the underside. Hard to tell."

"Not bad. Not bad," says St. Peter, writing in the big book. "A nine and a half. His pineal?"

The angel makes a loose fist, places it between Guy's brows, puts his lips to it, and sucks once, hard. He takes what looks like a cat's eye marble from his lips and wipes it on his gown, holds it up and looks at it. "A little murky. Not much mileage on it. Five on a scale of ten maybe."

"Okay, so look," St. Peter says, addressing Guy, "you're an average guy, Guy. What if we sent you back, threw you back like a fish?"

Guy thrilled at the thought!

And that's how Guy was born to Señor Eduardo Hughes and Señora Ester Roosen of Montevideo, Uruguay, nine months later. Eight pounds, seven ounces. They named him Eduardo after his father and Galeano after his mother's family name, and worried that his head was shaped like a plantain, but the doctors told them everything would be all right, that his head would get round in a few days' time and then they could worry about other things.

FORTUNE

Tommy, Tommy, Tommy. Here. I'm planting these begonias here. I hope they take. I can't stay long. It looks like rain again. I stopped at your mother's grave, too, and left her some of them white mums she liked. I didn't plant hers, though, just set the pot in front of her side of the stone, by where her dates are carved, and come right over here. I brought you something. Let me dig a little hole here. Put it right in here and cover it up. There. It's yours. Now listen to this story while I get some rocks around this so the goddamned rain don't wash it out.

This happened yesterday. I'm coming out of SNAK-MART with my lotto ticket same as always, a buck a day except for Sundays. Hell, the four blocks there and back's the only exercise I get these days. And Berj, the Persian—he's about it for company. I buy my ticket and he smiles. "Have good one," he says. "You too," I tell him. What the hell. He's not a bad guy, just not much for conversation. SNAK-MART was Mickey Fields' back when you knew it, not no more. When Mickey's wife passed on, he left it to his son John. Him you would remember. Then later Mickey died and John sold out and moved away someplace. But to hell with it, Tommy, I'm not complaining, that's just how it is.

So listen. I'm standing in this little doorway there 'cause as I'm coming out the rain comes down, no warning or nothing. The goddamn street is boiling and the gutters are running and I look up and there's a straight line cutting right across the sky. It's dark as hell on one side, bright blue on the other. And the line is moving. Eerie, it was. Put me in mind of that time once when you were little, when the light went funny and you got shook and I said there was nothing to be scared of 'cause I'd read the papers and I knew it was an eclipse. And you wanted to know what an eclipse was and I tried my best to explain it but you were, hell, I think in kindergarten. I remember saying my head was the sun, and this fist was the earth, and this one was the moon, and I'm sure I got it all balled up, but it didn't matter. You only needed to know there *was* an explanation. Or maybe that your Daddy had one for you, I don't know.

But I'm way off track. There was this kid—I say kid, he was maybe twenty, T-shirt and jeans, a backpack—he comes out the store behind me, but he can't get the door open far because I'm standing there. So you know me—I'm even fatter now—I kind of squash myself against the wall till he gets out and pulls his backpack through. And then he sees the rain. So now there's two of us standing there.

And the kid is nervous. Rocking back and forth. I'm getting nervous too, you want to know the truth. We're right on top of each other and it's raining like all hell broke loose, and you know me, I'd never say nothing, but the kid don't smell too good. There's people in all the doorways and under all the awnings up and down across the street, but I can't hardly see them through the rain. Every once in a while there's a flash of lightning and the thunder is cracking and booming. Magnificent, it was.

Then it stops. Just like that. It must have kept on raining to the east—no, south, I guess. That line was still across the sky but it was farther off now, to my right, on the other side of the firehouse. And I tell you the rain shut off like that, like somebody'd turned off a goddamned spigot.

Right then, the kid asks do I have the time. Five thirty-five, I tell him.

"Shit!" he yells, and you know me, I jump, I don't like sudden noises, and he's gone.

There was a rainbow it turns out. Up in back of me where I couldn't see, but everybody across the street is shading their eyes and pointing up at it.

This car was coming around the curve there—you know where I mean, there by the bank—and the driver was kind of ducking down and looking up to see what everybody's pointing at, and by the time he saw the kid it was too late. He hit the brakes but the street was slick and the kid went down and the car slid over him and stopped.

I only ever heard things get that quiet once or twice before. The time the doctor give your mother and me your diagnosis, telling us the name for it and how rare it was and that the odds were you'd be gone before the year was out. And maybe again years later when I found your mother down the cellar by the washing machine. All you could hear was the goddamned windshield wipers screeching on the dry glass. I knew—everybody knew—the kid was dead.

They must have seen it from the firehouse 'cause the EMTs come right away to pull him out. I heard one say it took his face right off. I never saw that though, thank God. I was already close to throwing up, I was so shook.

I could hardly talk to the cop. The TV crew was there and I tried to tell them about that line that moved across the sky, and how fast the rain stopped, and the rainbow, and how all them things come together, and how the kid asked for the time and ran out, and the car, and all the stuff I just told you, but then they didn't put me on. I watched that night, on the eleven o'clock. They had some other guy who saw it on. He was saying things like, "The gray vehicle entered the intersection from the southwest," and "the pedestrian was crossing rapidly," bullshit like that, and it made me angry. Like you could make some sense of a thing like that by telling it cold, with the heart ripped out of it.

When the news goes off, at midnight, they pick the winning number. How do I explain this? You never seen it. We never let you stay up that late. There's this machine full of ping-pong balls with numbers on them popping around inside like crazy, like a popcorn popper. Then some young lady the money guys dress up in a slinky outfit opens a little gate and a ball pops up, and then another one, and then another till we got all seven numbers. Tommy, I tell you I sat there like it was a dream, one goddamned digit at a time, and I felt nothing. Anger, maybe. And disgust. Call me a fool but I don't want it, not no more. So here. To hell with it. Besides, it's yours. It's the goddamned family fortune.

INTERFERENCE

During that summer of 1960, when he was eleven, Gregory Kessler liked to go upstairs and sing into the window fan in his bedroom. He liked the funny way it made his voice sound and he imagined the words on the other side of the window, shredded into tiny pieces and blowing out over the neighborhood on the evening breeze. He pictured them like snow swirling across the street to Willy Hunsicker's house, second from the corner, where evenings Willy's mother would sit in an aluminum and canvas beach chair on the sidewalk with her stockings rolled down to her ankles, smoking a cigarette and reading the newspaper in the light from the streetlamp on the corner; or up the block on the breeze to Kenny and Neil Messinger's house with their father just waking to help put the younger kids to bed before he left for the Uptown Diner — "Breakfast 24 hrs" — and then the night shift at Eli Coal & Carbon. If the breeze were blowing just right, a few words might make it around the corner to where Margaret Fisher lived, where the roots of the horse chestnut tree heaved up the sidewalk so that walking by you were, for a moment, tall enough to see into her house. At school last year, in fifth grade, Gregory had been paired with Margaret for a procession on the Feast of the Immaculate Conception, and when she took his hand, he let himself feel all the things the songs on the radio, the songs he sang into the fan, were about.

And they called it puppy love.
Oh, I guess they'll never know
How a young heart really feels
And why I love her so.

Margaret was quiet and kept entirely to herself. Gregory was comfortable with her shyness. He himself preferred solitude to hanging around with the only two guys in the neighborhood his age: Willy Hunsicker, who outweighed him by thirty pounds and had once sat on him and made him eat a worm, and Chris Messinger, who made him nervous because he was always burning stuff—model cars, toy soldiers, and once, his little sister's doll—dousing things with lighter fluid and putting a match to them.

In Margaret's case, Gregory understood, her shyness probably had to do with her being the new kid. All the others in the class had been together since kindergarten, while Margaret had only arrived at St. Polycarp's the year before. Introducing her on the first day of fourth grade, Sister Mary Patricia told the class that Margaret had lived in New York, New Jersey, and Delaware before moving to Pennsylvania. Margaret blushed deeply, slipped lower in her seat, and clasped her hands tightly on her desk. For a while the kids tried to include her, then they taunted her, and finally they left her alone.

Margaret's dad drove a Royal White laundry truck standing up, with the steering wheel on the wrong side of the cab so he could leap from his truck, one-two and, with a skip and a jump, ring the doorbells with a brown paper package in his hands. "Cleaner than clean, ... " it said on the side of the truck, "fresher than fresh!" Tuesday mornings he came down Gregory's street, and sometimes in the summer Margaret was with him. Gregory'd arrange to be on the crumbling concrete steps of his house, filing and refiling his baseball cards by team, and within each team by batting average, or ERA for pitchers—each team a block with a rubber band around it. If Margaret was in the truck, he tried to jut out his jaw a bit and look serious, and if she noticed him, he gave her a little two-fingered John Wayne salute off his right eyebrow with just the slightest nod.

After the truck pulled away and stopped again farther up the street, Gregory would run up the stairs to his room to watch it from the window. Often his mother would poke her head in then to ask if he was okay and he would tell her that he was, sighing and rolling his eyes, or stretching the word "Ma-ahm" into two annoyed, derisive syllables.

"Well, if you're okay, I want you outside. It's too beautiful a day for you to be mooning around in your room, singing into the fan, for godsake."

Gregory winced and blushed. He'd thought the singing was private. Besides, he hadn't been singing just then. How much else did his mother understand? His yearning for Margaret? The coded initials he'd written on his brown paper book covers, their initials intertwined: GMKF?

"Go find your brother. I swear I don't know what to do with you."

Gregory's mother worked a half-shift of overtime on Tuesdays, eleven to three, at the linen mill, in addition to her regular forty hours. The boys' father, MIA in Korea, was presumed dead, and like any woman in her circumstance, she had no patience for hanging around doing nothing.

"Go! Go to the park. Go anywhere. Just get out of the house and go play for godsake!"

Gregory always knew where to find his brother Dougie in the summer. He and his friends would be by the river, on the bluff above the deep water where a thick braided rope hung from the branch of a huge honey locust. They'd be taking turns swinging out over the black water downstream from the rapids, letting go at the highest point, upward and out in a long, arced flight, accompanied by first a loud whoop and then a great splash. Then the rope would snake back to where the others fought to grab hold of it.

Most of the boys would twist and tumble through the air and try to end up tucked in a ball that made a dull *kaboom* and a tall column of water. Dougie, however, always managed to hit the water with a quick *rip* sound like a flat stone when it turns sideways and won't skip. That was even neater, and Dougie had offered to teach him, but Gregory was too scared — he looked down, heart pounding, and started shaking and backing away from the edge.

"Don't worry about it," Dougie told him. "You're still little. When you're bigger you'll do it." Gregory always heard "when you're bigger" as a taunt, coming from his brother, a reminder that Dougie was four years older, stronger and more powerful. Then Dougie swung out on the rope, let go, and Gregory watched as he entered the water clean as a blade.

Sometimes when they were both home, when no other kids were around, it was the way it used to be. They might sit on the floor on the braided rug and play rummy or crazy-8s, or drag the old electric football game from the closet and plug it in, choosing all-star teams and giving the little two-dimensional players the names of their favorite pros according to position.

Lately though, Dougie was making it clear that he'd rather be with almost anybody but his little brother, maybe because he was often left in charge for short periods when his mother had to run some errand or another, and that always meant he had to stay home unless he wanted to take Gregory with him when he met up with his friends — and that was worse.

"Mom, that's not fair! Besides, he's not a baby. He can take care of himself!"

Gregory's hurt feelings on these occasions were offset by gratitude that his brother'd said he wasn't "a baby." The trouble was that, other times, with his friends especially, that's what Dougie called him, "a baby." For his own part, Gregory resented the fact that Dougie was the one who got new clothes, new toys, new sports equipment, while everything he had was something Dougie had grown out of.

Gregory went out through the back door and hopped on his bike to ride to the river. Why did his mother have to be like that? Couldn't she see he was practically a teenager? That eleven is a teen even if you don't say it that way? Sometimes he just wanted to stay in his room and think. About Margaret mostly. He liked to lie on his bed and imagine they were kissing; he would hug the pillow to his chest and press his thumb into his lips. Sometimes he nuzzled the soft blond hairs on his arm and imagined they were the downy gold at the nape of her neck. He let the songs play in his head. He longed for romance, heartbreak, heroism; he yearned to be grown up and in love.

> *Venus if you will*
> *Please send a little girl for me to thrill.*
> *A girl who wants my kisses and my arms*
> *A girl with all the charms of you.*

He cut across the abandoned lumberyard and parked his bike near the hole in the chain-link fence topped with rusty barbed wire and covered with honeysuckle, ragged and sweet. He could hear they were there. He liked the quality of sound of the place, the rumble of trucks on the bridge, the way the sheer rock face on the other side echoed their voices, on some days more than others. Just through the fence was a boulder on which he could climb and see his brother and the others for a moment, and then he was on the dirt path that switchbacked several times through the high weeds alive with grasshoppers and other chirring insects.

One of Dougie's friends, Kenny Messinger, saw him first. "Hey Doug. Doug. Check it out. Snotboy's here!"

Gregory tried to smile, as if this were a nickname, as if he were being welcomed. It was the usual crowd of Dougie's friends: Kenny; Kenny's twin, Neil; Zack; and Sam, all boys he'd known his whole life, neighbors, but somehow strangers now. Like Dougie, they had no use for him. These days he felt ashamed in their presence. They called him birdboy for his bony chest and skinny legs. They had all "filled out" as his mother called it. Muscular and hairy, they punched each other hard, so you could hear fists thumping shoulders, their voices deep and loud.

A new sign at the end of the path read "SWIM AT YOUR OWN RISK, Town of Norville, Dept. of Parks." It replaced the weathered "NO SWIMMING" sign, covered with the carved initials of generations of teenaged boys, that had been there until this year.

As Gregory approached, Zack cut loose with his loudest Tarzan yell as he let go of the rope; his cry ended in a loud smack as he hit the water. The echo sounded like a slap. "Oooww, that hurt!" said Neil, shaking his head to the side to drain water from his ear. When Zack surfaced, they all taunted him.

"Oh man, instant sunburn!"

"Down in flames, man!"

"Hey, check and make sure your nuts are still there!"

"Offer it up for the souls in purgatory!"

Zack scrabbled up the rocks and exposed roots of the bluff to stand again on the packed earth. His face, chest, stomach and thighs were all a bright red. "What are you lookin' at, dick-lick?" He was speaking to Gregory. "Well?"

"Lay off, Zack," Dougie said from the edge of the cliff where he'd managed to get hold of the rope. He backed up several steps to get a good running start.

Gregory saw it coming, but there was no way to avoid it: as soon as Dougie was in the air over the river, Zack and the others were on him. "Red-belly! Grab him!" Gregory was on the ground, his T-shirt pulled over his head, a woody root cutting into his shoulder blade, the twins pinning his arms. He tried to kick, but Sam was soon sitting on his shins and holding his knees together and Zack was smacking his stomach, leading the chant: "Red-belly, red-belly, red-belly."

By the time Dougie had climbed out of the water the assault was over and Zack had pushed Neil aside, grabbed the rope, and was set to swing out over the water again. "Hey, Dougie, tell your little homo brother that's the way we deal with chickenshitters. Ride the rope, you little homo, or go home to your mommy!"

Holding his hot and tingling belly, Gregory could feel the rising welts left by Zack's hands. Dougie grabbed him by the arm and said in a clenched whisper, "Why do you just let them do this? Why don't you fight? What's the matter with you?"

"Like I had a chance."

"Oh, come on, don't be such a baby. Nobody made you come here."

"Mom did."

"Yeah, well, Mom's not gonna fight your battles for you, is she?"

Gregory pulled away to walk up through the field to his bike. Zack hit the water with a great thumping splash that echoed as a string of dying bass percussions, joined by the other boys' cheers.

When Gregory returned to the fence, he saw the laundry truck in the lumberyard, but his wondering at it was trumped by the realization that his bike was not where he had left it. He ran along the fence this way and that, looking to see if someone had maybe hidden it as a joke, but it was gone. Gone! There was no sense in telling his brother and the others. How would he tell his mother? He'd begged her for that bike instead of Dougie's old one. He let the tears come and kicked at the fence, tearing handful after handful of honeysuckle from the chain-link until a cloying sweetness filled the air.

"What's wrong, son?"

Gregory spun around. It was Margaret's father, standing right behind him in his white uniform; he was holding a camera with the biggest, longest lens Gregory had ever seen fastened around his neck by a strap. Gregory turned back to face the fence; he felt humiliated. Margaret's father! And here he was sniffling like a baby.

"Nothing."

"Nothing?"

"I'm sorry. I mean nothing, Mr. Fisher." And now he was showing his bad manners, too!

"No, no. That's not what I meant, son. I mean is there anything I can do for you is all."

Gregory turned to face the man. "Somebody stole my bike."

"Are you sure? 'Cause I've been here awhile now." He raised the camera. "Taking pictures of the birds. You like birds?"

Gregory toed the dirt, still trying to pull himself together. Fisher handed him a folded handkerchief, and Gregory blew his nose in it and then didn't know what to do with it.

"You just keep that."

"I have allergies," Gregory said. "They make my eyes water and I have to blow my nose."

"Yeah, bad time of year for that." He was looking through the camera at the bridge, adjusting the telephoto lens. "What color was this bike of yours? Blue?"

"Yes, sir."

"With a basket on the front?"

"Yes, sir."

"And colored streamers on the handgrips?"

"Yes, sir!"

"Come on! Get in the truck, let's get you your bike back."

"Did you see him? Did you take his picture?"

"Come on, come on! We don't want to lose him. No. Go around the other side." Fisher started the truck and it whined when he put it in reverse. Gregory sat on a high, torn leather seat with the stuffing coming out of it. There was a handle to grab hold of in the doorway. Fisher kept his left hand on the knob of the long gearshift that rose from the middle of the corrugated metal floor and bent at an angle. They lurched forward.

"Now, listen," Fisher shouted over the engine. He shifted. "If we catch this guy, you leave it up to me, you understand?"

Gregory was noticing everything about the truck: the big, flat twin-paned windshield with wiper blades up top that had swept two boxy smiles in the dust; the small yellowing plastic Virgin on the dashboard; a clipboard holding a fat wad of pink and white papers; more papers tucked up under the visor in front of him. He had an exciting sense that he was in Margaret's world now, riding in this truck he watched for on Tuesdays, hearing its predictable whine and the sound of its braking as it made its way down his street toward and then away from his house. It was a strange sensation being inside all that familiar noise.

"You understand?" shouted Fisher.

Gregory looked at him. He had a ruddy face, high forehead, bony nose, and a protruding vein that curled like a purple worm from his brow to his crew cut.

"I mean it. I know you must be angry, but I saw this kid and believe me, he's no match for a guy like you." He spoke loudly, eyes on the road. "A guy as strong as you would tear him limb from limb."

Gregory knew he wasn't strong; at least he didn't feel strong. Still, Margaret's father seemed to think he was. Maybe he would go home and tell Margaret how he met a big strong friend of hers today, how together they had caught a thief and made him give his bike back.

As if he were reading Gregory's thoughts, Fisher said, "We're a team now. So listen to me, son. This is going to be clean. We catch up to him and tell him we know the bike is yours. We put the bike in the back of the truck and turn around. And that's all." They rumbled over the bridge; he could see downstream to where one of the twins, Kenny or Neil, had just swung out over the water and let go.

A little way past the bridge, they turned onto a narrow road that ran beside a cemetery. Fisher slowed. "There she is." He pointed with a movement of his chin. The bike stood there, propped on its kickstand, conveniently in a turnout big enough for the truck. "Don't seem like anyone's around," said Fisher as they pulled onto the dirt and gravel. Gregory wondered where the kid who stole it would have gone; there was nothing to do around here. "Stay here." Fisher hopped down, opened the back doors, put the bike in, and slammed the doors shut.

As they pulled back onto the road, Fisher reached across the open cab and tousled Gregory's hair. "What a team we make," he said. "A regular Batman and Robin. What do you say, Boy Wonder? You've been through a lot. You want to stop off for some ice cream? My treat."

Gregory thought that sounded good. He shrugged.

Fisher lightly slapped Gregory's thigh. "I would say you really proved yourself today. A lot of young men, even older than you, would have panicked when they saw their bike was gone, but you kept your head on your shoulders. I like that in a guy." He gave Gregory's shoulder a pat before he shifted into fourth gear.

Gregory wondered what he'd done besides ride in the truck, but he was also thinking how great it was that Margaret's father thought so well of him. One day, when they were older, when the time came for him to ask Margaret to marry him, her father would think it was a neat thing. Who cared about Zack and his brother's friends and the stupid rope and all that babyish stuff? The wind blew warm on his face as he let a song play in his head:

> *When I want you in my arms*
> *When I want you and all your charms*
> *Whenever I want you*
> *All I have to do is dream, dream, dream.*

That evening Gregory sang every song he knew into the fan, some of them more than once. Unsettled and nervous, he sang to calm himself, all the while turning over and over the idea of himself as a kid — a guy — with special qualities, a thought that he liked. Margaret's father liked and respected him. Maybe Margaret would be his girlfriend. His brother and his friends could have their stupid rope and stand around punching one another like a bunch of knuckleheads. He was soon to be in love and all you had to do was turn on the radio to know that everything was better and that life was hardly worth living if you weren't in love.

He imagined his voice like colored confetti carrying farther than ever, beyond the neighborhood, over the river, out of town.

The following Tuesday Gregory waited on the front steps until the laundry truck came down the street. He was disappointed to discover that Margaret was not in it. Fisher dropped off some laundry next door and waved to Gregory. "Want to ride along and give me a hand there, partner? I don't guess we'll rescue any bicycles today, but I could use some help with my route."

Gregory grabbed up his various piles of baseball cards, collecting them in one block, and put a rubber band around it. "I have to ask my mom."

She was getting ready for work, pinning her hair up. When he asked her she gave herself a stern look in the mirror, sighed, and came to the front door. Gregory hadn't told her anything about the bike; he could not have said why he hadn't, but he knew, somehow, that he shouldn't. She would probably have scolded him for leaving the bike someplace where he couldn't keep an eye on it.

"Afternoon, Ma'am," Fisher said. "I wondered if my young friend here might ride along in the truck and give me a hand with some of these bundles."

Gregory gave his mother a pleading look. She appeared uncertain and agitated.

"And you are?" she asked, squinting a bit.

Fisher instantly thrust out his hand. "Karl Fisher, Ma'am. I live close by, right there around the corner, in fact. You have a fine young man here. Fine young man." He almost put his hand on Gregory's shoulder, but changed his mind.

"He's eleven. He's an eleven-year-old boy, Mr. Fisher."

Why did she say that? Gregory thought. Why does she have to make me out to be such a baby?

"And a fine one," said Fisher.

"You two know each other?"

Gregory caught Fisher's eye and said, "I go to school with Margaret. She's Mr. Fisher's daughter." He could see surprise on Fisher's face that he hadn't told his mother about the bike. Then Fisher's face became approving, even, Gregory thought, admiring.

"Of course, of course. It's coming back to me now. You sometimes usher at the ten o'clock Mass, if I'm not mistaken."

"First and third Sundays of the month. Knights of Columbus. So many want to pass the basket, we have to rotate. But as I said, I sure could use a hand. My Margaret is at some Girl Scout thing this afternoon, and I've got extra bundles to deliver."

While Fisher was speaking, Gregory watched his mother's face change as she recalled that he was a widower raising his daughter alone. Gregory had once heard her talking with Mrs. Hunsicker after Mass. "Lord knows — and so do I — it isn't easy," she'd said, "you've got to hand it to him."

Fisher looked at his watch. "I'm already running late."

"Please please, Mom. Please?"

His mother smiled. "He's such a dreamy boy, I guess it would be good for him."

Why, why did his mother have to say things like that? How could she not be aware of how embarrassing her comments were? Were his feelings so unimportant to her? She was doing that thing that adults always did — talking about him as if he wasn't there, and as if he were a prize houseplant who needed just the right amounts of sun and water.

That's what I like about Margaret's father, thought Gregory. He's different. He sees who I am. Even right now, for example, he's looking right at me. He can see my mother is embarrassing me. At the same time, a tiny wave of fear went through him and he could not hold the man's gaze. It didn't make sense but he worried that somehow, in his shame at his mother's remark, he had been rendered as transparent as he felt — after all, it was this man's daughter he was often so dreamy about.

"I'm sure he'll be a big help, Mrs. Kessler."

"Well, you let me know if he gives you any trouble."

Fisher put his hand on Gregory's shoulder and with a gentle

twist turned him toward the truck. "I'll have him back in time for supper, then. We'd better get moving; we're losing time. Thanks, Mrs. Kessler."

For the whole first hour or so they hardly spoke. Fisher hopped in and out of the truck three or four times each block, popping in for a bundle, throwing a sack of clothes to be laundered in a wire bin in the back of the truck. Gregory started to get bored and wished he'd brought his transistor radio; then he started to worry that maybe he'd done something wrong. Finally, Fisher leaned across and punched his upper arm. "Know what I like about you?"

Gregory shrugged.

"You're your own man. I've been thinking. You never mentioned any of that bike business to your mother, did you? I could see that right away. Know what? That's what I like. A boy's adventures are a boy's adventures and nobody's business but his own, I say. You? I see you understand that."

Gregory liked his way of looking at it. It wasn't that he was afraid to tell, it was that he didn't want his mother "minding his beeswax," as she herself would have put it. Here was a grown-up who seemed to understand him better than he understood himself.

"I'll tell you something else I think you know already." They were coming down a steep hill and Fisher ground the gears a bit downshifting. The truck stuttered and Gregory rocked forward and braced himself on the dash. "Your mother doesn't mean to embarrass you. She just can't help herself. One thing about mothers, son — they were never boys. Mothers love you and want what's best for you, but they've never been boys. So listen to your mother, son, but listen carefully because — and this is what I really like about you, that even at your age you know this — when she tries to talk to you about guy stuff, she don't know a thing about it. Am I right? You know that, don't you?"

Gregory felt certain that he did know this, just as Fisher said, although he'd never really thought about it. He nodded.

"Okay, then." Fisher was pulling alongside Veterans Park with its monument and lawns and flowerbeds and band shell. "You jump out here and wait for me. I have to load for the afternoon deliveries and you can't come. I'll bring you some pizza when I come back. All right?"

Gregory nodded. As the truck whined off, Gregory sat in the shade, leaning against the band shell, feeling the cool concrete through the thin cotton of his T-shirt. He watched a robin working the lawn in front of him, hopping and stabbing at the ground with its beak. Now he really wished he'd remembered to bring his radio. He lost the shade after a while and had to move to a cooler spot. When he was about out of his mind with boredom, the truck pulled up and Fisher beeped the horn.

"You like Grape Nehi?" Fisher asked him as he handed him the slice of pizza.

The afternoon was different. Gregory rode in the back of the truck. Fisher would call out a name to him and Gregory would find the brown package with the name on it in crayon. It was fun. There was a rhythm to it on certain streets where the laundry had lots of customers. Whenever Fisher returned to the truck he would heave a cotton sack of laundry at Gregory who caught it, staggering, and worked at pretending it wasn't heavy.

"Everything under control back there?" Fisher would yell above the noise of the truck.

At the end of the day, back in the neighborhood, Fisher dropped Gregory at his house. "Hey!" he said as Gregory was getting out of the truck, "don't you want your pay?" He handed Gregory a five-dollar bill, which was the most money Gregory had ever held in his eleven-year-old hand.

"You want to work some more tomorrow?"

Gregory nodded, holding the bill at both ends, astonished.

"Put that away somewhere; that's just between the two of us. And listen: you're worth every penny of that pay, you hear? But you can't tell anybody I gave it to you. If they find out down at the laundry that I'm paying you, then they'll think that I can't handle the work myself and I might lose my job. I'll pick you up just after nine."

Dinner was something his mother made out of tuna and egg noodles. Dougie put ketchup and salt and pepper on it; Dougie put ketchup and salt and pepper on everything his mother cooked. His mother sat and spooned herself a helping. "Did you have fun riding in the truck, Gregory?"

"Wha' truck?" Dougie asked through a mouthful.

"Gregory's made a friend. One of his schoolmates' fathers is the laundry man. You must have seen his truck around town."

"Yeah, like wherever me and my friends go! He's like a spy or something. We look up and there's his truck. The guy's a creep."

"Is not," said Gregory.

"Is too."

"Is not."

"Is too and so are you!"

"Stop it. The two of you stop it right now!" She turned to Gregory. "Where did you go?"

Gregory was moving things around with his fork, trying to separate the tuna and the celery from the noodles and make three piles so he could eat each ingredient one at a time.

"Mom! Make him stop! I can't stand it when he does that!"

"Mind your business then and don't look."

Gregory was thinking about the different neighborhoods where they'd picked up and delivered laundry and Veterans Park where he'd sat in the shade. He shrugged. "All over. Everywhere," he said.

"See?" Mrs. Kessler said, looking at Dougie.

"See what?"

"He has deliveries all over town. Or maybe you think he's a communist spy, paid by the Russians to watch you and your friends ride your bikes?"

"He's a perv, Mom. Zack caught him taking pictures of us swimming."

"He takes pictures of birds, stupid! Birds! He showed me some."

"Yeah. Did you ever see his daughter? What a retard! She looks like a zombie! An albino zombie!" Dougie made a monster face at Gregory, pulling down his lower lids with two fingers and pushing up a pig nose.

All in one motion Gregory stood and swiped all his food off his plate at Dougie. "Is NOT!"

"That's it! Both of you! Gregory, you will clean this up right now and Douglas, you will stay in your room the rest of this evening. Now move!"

"Is too-oo," sang Dougie as he left the table.

Wednesday they made deliveries on the north side of town, across the river. It was suburban there: lawns and trees, flagstone walks and decorative lamp posts. When Fisher came back to the truck he sometimes seemed winded. He had a handkerchief around his neck and his face was red and sweaty. It was hot in the back of the truck, but Gregory didn't mind. He'd brought his transistor radio and earplug and sometimes he could listen to a whole song before Fisher came back with a bag of laundry for him.

This time for lunch Fisher had made them bologna sandwiches and bought Cokes from a machine at a filling station. "I know a great spot," said Fisher. "Come on, ride up front now; it's hotter'n a whorehouse on payday back there." He smiled.

Gregory only understood the hot part but he smiled back. Why was Fisher looking at him and shaking his head? Did he do something wrong?

"I swear you are the best assistant I ever had!"

Gregory wanted to ask about Margaret. Wasn't she a good assistant?

"Most things that are worthwhile doing require an assistant, somebody you can trust, somebody smart and loyal and fun to be with. Somebody who likes to learn." They had pulled onto a gravel road outside of town. "Even some things that are not worthwhile require an assistant, like this stupid job."

Gregory could see they were following the river; he could hold onto the handle and lean way out the door and look at himself in the tall sideview mirror and see the great cloud of dust billowing behind them.

"So. Do you? Like to learn things. How do you do in school?"

Gregory shrugged. He didn't want to talk about school. Grown-ups always wanted to talk about school. He felt a little wave of disappointment in Fisher.

"Because I'll tell you what I've been thinking. You're a great laundry assistant, a good worker, and you don't complain all the time like some people."

Gregory thought he must be referring to Margaret.

"But see the thing is, I don't know if you have what it takes to be a good photography assistant."

Gregory wanted to say, "Yes, yes I do!" but he wasn't sure what it took, only that he wanted to do it.

"You have to be smart. And you have to be honest. Here we are." He pulled off into a little clearing where there was a picnic table by the river. A tall weeping willow grew in a nearly perfect dome at the water's edge. Fisher turned off the truck, sat back, and gave Gregory an appraising look.

"I do good in school," Gregory said.

Fisher smiled. "Grab that bag behind your seat," he said. It was Fisher's camera and photographic gear. It was heavy as Gregory carried it to the picnic table; it hung below his knees and he struggled not to trip over it. The canvas strap cut into his shoulder, but he did his best to make it look easy for him. He hoisted it up onto the picnic table. Fisher seemed pleased with him.

As they sat there eating their sandwiches, Fisher began to remove items from the bag: the camera, a piece of red cloth, a large brown accordion folder, and several lenses he arranged in graduating order of length on the table. He finished his sandwich quickly and began dusting the lenses with the red cloth. "The thing about photography is that a photograph never lies. A picture of a bird's the bird in that moment when you shoot him. It's a little like hunting, except you don't kill anything. You don't have to stuff it and mount it to bring it home with you. They say that in a few years time, we'll all be using color film like the magazines do. Won't that be something? Here, look at this." He slid a black-and-white photo of a bird from the envelope. "This goldfinch. I've got him right here. We've got him right here. But that bird flew away the minute I took that picture and he's someplace else now, just going on with his finchy life. You understand?"

Gregory nodded.

"And no matter what happens to that bird after that, if it gets eaten by a cat, or gets sick and dies. Well, we still have this picture of him to admire like this, in private. And the bird doesn't even know you have its picture. Not that it would care. It's like having a secret. Like knowing something nobody else knows. You see?"

Gregory thought it only mostly made sense to him, but he couldn't think what part to ask about. He nodded.

"Unless you show it to somebody else, see? Like you know this bird here now. How you can almost know what color it is by looking at it carefully." Fisher looked him in the eye, unblinking, for a long moment.

"Does this mean I'm your assistant?" Caught in the man's gaze, it was the only question Gregory could formulate to ask.

"Depends." Fisher rose, attaching a medium-size lens onto his camera. "It's not a little thing, an assistant. You have to be willing to learn. It's not just about cameras and lenses and carrying bags. We'll have to wait and see. Tell you what. While I shoot some birds, why don't you sort out those pictures in the envelope for me? Just put the pictures of each kind of bird together in a stack. Don't worry you don't know the names of them, just put the like ones in a stack, like playing solitaire, okay?" He headed off toward the water.

A sparrow landed on the bench and hopped up on the table where it pecked at crumbs from Fisher's sandwich, then flew away. Gregory carefully took the thick stack of photos from the folder.

The one on top was a bird with a straight pointy bill. He guessed it was a kind of woodpecker and placed it next to the finch on the table. Though the birds were all gray in the photographs, there were differences: some had a bit of white along the wings or tail, others a black stripe across the eye or a tuft or crest of feathers on their heads. He made a little pile for each. He recognized robins and sparrows and jays, and he knew cardinals and orioles from his baseball card collection. He kept the piles in rows so Fisher would see how neat he could be.

He picked up another photo of the bird that Fisher had called a goldfinch and under it was a very different picture: in this one a man and woman faced the camera, naked; the woman sat on the man's lap and — his thing was in her thing! Her head was thrown back and the man was smiling at the camera, his chin over her right shoulder, his left hand cupping her breast. The whole bottom third of the stack were shots like this, of people coupling in various positions. Gregory's heart raced and thumped the way it had when he stood with Dougie at the top of the bluff, although the feeling wasn't fear exactly, and he didn't want to back away. He tried to recall what he'd heard about this. He was curious about what the people in the photos were doing and curious about the pictures' effect on him. He thought he might cry, but he didn't feel sad, and at the same time he felt like he might laugh, though nothing was funny. It was like being tickled, just before you yell "Stop!" He looked ahead, his hands shaking, at picture after picture.

"Smile!" said Fisher, and snapped the photo just as Gregory looked up. He lowered the camera on his way to the table. "What! What the devil? You're not supposed to be looking at these!" He picked up the stack of them. "Oh my lord, son, I'm sorry. You're not supposed to see these. I had no idea these were in there. These are private, you understand? Private."

Gregory sat with his head down, his hands on the bench under his thighs, his face hot, trying to calm himself.

"What's the matter, son? Oh, you're worried about that photograph I took when you were looking at the dirty picture, aren't you? Listen, you don't need to worry about that. I'll never show that photograph to anybody, not your mother, not the sisters at the school, nobody. I promise."

Gregory felt panic; it hadn't occurred to him that he was caught on film, captured like a bird, looking at the forbidden pictures.

"Look, son. I'm being honest with you. You remember I said that an assistant has to be honest? Well then, you deserve to be treated the same way. You still want to be my assistant, don't you?"

Gregory nodded.

"Okay then. Neither of us will say anything about these pictures. To anybody. Honest. Honest?"

"Honest," said Gregory.

"You have to understand. Just like I told you, there's a lot to learn growing up. Those pictures are guy stuff. A man might sometimes like to be alone with pictures like these, well, maybe to study them, like you study those pictures of the birds. You see?"

Gregory said yes, an assistant needs to be smart.

"This must be a shock to you, a boy raised by his mother."

Gregory thought for a moment. Mothers aren't guys. They don't know a thing about it!

"Now think about it," Fisher went on. "People will try to say there's something wrong with pictures like these. But what does it hurt these people in the pictures? They're off doing whatever they're doing now, don't even know you looked at them."

Just like goldfinches.

"And a man might feel some very strong feelings looking at these. Good, powerful feelings." He had been holding the packet of photos at arms length, now he brought them to his chest. "You'll feel those feelings when you get bigger."

Wait! Gregory wanted to protest. I did feel those things! Once again, it seemed as if Fisher were reading his mind. "Oh. Oh boy. Now I see," said Fisher. "You're more of a man than I thought. You felt some of that already, so you think you know what I'm talking about, am I right?"

Gregory felt terribly transparent, as if there was nothing he could possibly hide from Fisher.

"Well, you don't. You understand? You don't! You've got a lot to learn." Fisher looked at his watch. "Time to move out, soldier."

That afternoon when he dropped off Gregory and gave him his five-dollar bill, Fisher seemed reluctant to look at him. "Tell you what. Take a few days off now. I'll pick you up Tuesday morning when I'm back around here."

Gregory wanted to protest so badly he had to take care not to cry, but he turned to his boring house where he lived with his nosey mother and stupid brother and, wondering if he was being punished for something, walked up the broken steps. He waved to Fisher as he pulled away but Fisher didn't wave back.

"How's your commie pervert friend?" Dougie said as he came through the door.

"Shut up, stupid."

"I heard the Russians have pictures of every little kid in America so they can follow them around and kidnap the stupid ones — that would be you — for ransom money to build more nuclear missiles."

"That's dumb. Besides, I'm not a little kid!"

"I'll bet old Cleaner-than-Clean already took your picture, didn't he?"

Gregory blushed.

"See. It's probably already on its way to Moscow."

"Is not."

Dougie drew a finger across his throat, rolled back his eyes, and made gagging and dying sounds. "I tried to warn you!" he yelled after Gregory, who was already heading upstairs.

In his room, Gregory flopped on his bed and turned on his transistor. Roy Orbison matched his mood:

> *Only the lonely*
> *Know the way I feel tonight.*

Only the lonely
Know this feeling ain't right.

He soon convinced himself that he was pining for Margaret, but when he closed his eyes he kept seeing the people in the private photographs that he wasn't supposed to see in the first place, that he shouldn't have looked at, and he felt shaky inside and hot and very confused.

The whole next day, Thursday, those people returned to his thoughts whenever he was quiet, and once he almost wiped out on his bike when he hit a deep pothole that he had always steered around before. He found himself looking at people, grown-ups, and imagining them naked, in positions like the ones in the pictures. He felt like a spy. It was just like Fisher had said: like having a secret no one else knows; it was exciting, and it didn't hurt anybody; everybody just went on about their business.

Friday he rode his bike on the sidewalk past Margaret's house, standing up on the pedals as he coasted over the root-broken sidewalk and looking into the house, but no one was home.

Saturday it rained all day. Dougie went over to Kenny and Neil's. His mother tried to get him to take Gregory, but neither of the boys would hear of it.

"You're going to mope around in your room all day again?"

"Ma-ahm!"

"What is the matter with you? You've hardly eaten a thing for days. You don't go out. You don't talk. I'm just worried you're getting sick."

"I'm fine, Ma. Just quit it."

He lay on his bed all that afternoon, flushed and sweating as if with a fever, remembering the people in the pictures and animating them in his imagination — excitement, fear, and shame licking over him like flames.

Sunday was Mass, the ten o'clock this week because Dougie was scheduled to serve. Next year Gregory would be old enough to begin training. He already knew most of the Latin responses from helping Dougie memorize them.

> *Introibo ad altare Dei.*
> *"Ad Deum qui laetificat juventutem meam."*

During the Offertory, men strode from the back of the church with long-handled wicker baskets on their shoulders like rifles, two down the center aisle and one down each side; with the precision of a color guard, they genuflected in unison, then began working the rows with their baskets, collecting the envelopes, labeled according to the liturgical calendar and numbered for identification. Fisher was with them, collecting from rows on the other side of the church. Gregory's envelope, gendered blue, said "My Offering," with a boy and girl kneeling in prayer, their guardian angels bending over them. He dropped it in the basket with a five-dollar bill inside, a self-imposed penance for his dirty thoughts. He prayed, hard, to be forgiven for his new sin. He was sorry for looking at the pictures and sorry for remembering them over and over.

Monday Gregory slept late and woke up wanting to cry. It was strange and even scary to feel so sad first thing in the morning and without even knowing why. Maybe it was because the day before, as he and his mother were leaving Mass, he had seen Margaret next to her father in the vestibule and, when he said "Hi," she turned and looked at him in a way that absolutely paralyzed him. He had never seen a look of such cold, impersonal hatred, ever, on anyone, and he thought she must be angry at him because he'd taken her place as her father's assistant. He wanted to tell her he was sorry, but he wanted to be her father's assistant; couldn't they both be assistants? Couldn't they be assistants together? All day he thought of riding his bike around the corner to see her, to tell her he was sorry, to let her see how much he cared for her:

Venus if you do
I promise that I always will be true.
I'll give her all the love I have to give
As long as we both shall live.

But he couldn't. He could hardly move. While his mother was at work, he lay on the sofa, without even listening to his transistor. When she came home, she asked him if he was sick. "I'm just tired out, Ma," he said.

"What've you been doing all day?"

"Nothing, Ma. I'm just tired, that's all."

"Well, how a boy can get so tired doing nothing is beyond me." She sat down on a chair, took off her shoes, and rubbed her tired feet one after the other. At dinner Dougie talked enthusiastically about Zack stepping on a board with a nail in it and how it went right through his sneaker and all the way through his foot and out the other side, but Gregory felt as if he was hearing Dougie from far away. He hardly ate anything. Right after dinner he went back to his room and sat by the fan with the transistor earplug in his ear, listening to song after song without really hearing them or having even once the urge to sing along. In fact, he felt so numb he tried to conjure up the pictures again, the men and women doing shocking and thrilling things, hoping to wake an excitement he could recall but no longer feel.

Tuesday Gregory wore his cargo shorts so he could carry his transistor radio and earplug in the side pocket. He waited on the front steps and heard the truck before it turned the corner, headed down the street, and stopped in front of his house.

"Well, come on!" Fisher said.

The morning's work did not go well. Twice Fisher asked him what in the hell was wrong with him. He was slow retrieving the brown paper packages from the back, and once Fisher knocked him over heaving a bag of laundry at him. "Pay attention! Pay attention!"

At lunchtime they headed back out on the river road. Gregory held onto the door handle and leaned out as before, watching the road dust billow out behind them like smoke. The sky was clouding over and it looked like rain.

"Want to play questions?" Fisher yelled across the cab to him.

Gregory sat back down in his seat. "Okay."

"I figure to work together we ought to know each other a bit more. What is it your mama does all day?"

"She works."

"I know. I know. But where's she work?"

"At the linen mill."

"Okay, your turn."

Gregory wanted to ask about the things the people were doing in the photographs and he wanted to understand why it was so exciting to look at them. Instead he asked, "Are you a communist?"

"A communist! Now why would I be a communist?"

Gregory shrugged.

"Who says I'm a communist? Did somebody call me that?"

Suddenly Gregory felt he had betrayed his brother. "No."

"Okay, my turn. Okay then, what else have you heard about me? Anything?"

"That you take pictures of kids to send to the Russians so they can figure out who to kidnap for ransom."

Fisher laughed so hard he nearly drove off the road. "Now why would I do that? Now why," he could hardly control his laughter and he reached across and squeezed Gregory's thigh, hard, "why would I do that? You've seen the kind of pictures I like to take."

He pulled the truck into the small picnic area. Along with their lunchbag he carried a canvas Army surplus dispatch bag. "You want the ham or the baloney?"

"Baloney, please."

"Let me ask you something else," said Fisher as he took a bite of the ham sandwich. "You didn't say anything about these pictures here to anybody, right?" He rested his hand on the canvas bag.

Gregory shook his head; clearly Fisher did not mean the pictures of birds. "No. No sir," he said. "I promised. I'm honest." Just knowing those other pictures were in the bag thrilled him. He felt his face flush and he tried to pretend disinterest. The bag had been behind the driver's seat so he could have looked at the pictures lots of times that morning while Fisher was out of the truck — if he had only known! He was suddenly hungry and tore into his sandwich with an awakened appetite.

"All right then. Then I've got a good assistant, somebody I can trust."

Gregory took a slug of Orange Crush. Fisher was staring at him. The purple vein on Fisher's forehead seemed to writhe under his skin when he chewed. A few fat drops of rain splatted on the picnic table, then there was thunder, and in another moment the rain was coming down in earnest. Fisher got up, looked around, and headed toward the willow's shelter, calling back to Gregory. "Gather up that stuff and bring it along here. Hurry up. Let's get in out of the rain!" Gregory gathered up his lunch and the canvas bag and followed Fisher to the river and through the hanging boughs and under the willow's canopy.

It may have been when they began to look at the photos again, together, Fisher using words that Gregory had never heard before; or when Fisher began to touch him; or when he began to want a way out; or when they came to the photographs of Margaret, naked, with three naked men. It may have been when Fisher pressed him backward, gently, to the ground and then, not so gently, held him there, or it may have been what happened after that. In any case, it was there, with the willow weeping all around them, that the noise began that Gregory would carry in his head forever after, so harsh it was soft, so loud it was quiet, like rushing water or like the place on the radio dial between two stations, a muffled roar through which you could sometimes hear faint voices, though not what they were singing.

ACKNOWLEDGMENTS

These stories have appeared in the following periodicals, sometimes in slightly different versions:

> *Ascent*: "Gentlemen"
> *Bostonia*: "From This Distance, At This Speed"
> *Iconoclast*: "Lucky Garden"
> *The Larcom Review*: "Are You with Me?"
> *The Marlboro Review*: "Fortune"
> *Post Road*: "Nothing to Look at Here"
> *The Sun*: "Sugar"
> *Witness*: "Harvey's Birthday" and "Interference"
> *Words & Images*: "Burning Bright"

The author wishes to thank the Massachusetts Cultural Council for two grants that provided assistance in the writing of these stories.

Essential peace and quiet was provided by David Rosner and Ellen Schutz, and by Lee Hope Betcher and Bill Betcher, who kindly provided their homes as retreats from the world of obligations. Thanks also to Kathleen Aguero, Frederick Reiken, W. Scott Olsen, and Mako Yoshikawa for keen editorial advice.

BIOGRAPHY

Richard Hoffman is author of the award-winning *Half the House: A Memoir*, and the poetry collections *Without Paradise* and *Gold Star Road*, which was awarded the Barrow Street Press Poetry Prize and won the New England Poetry Club's 2009 Sheila Motton Award for the best book of poetry published in the past two years. His writing, both prose and verse, has appeared in *Agni, Ascent, Harvard Review, Hudson Review, Poetry, Post Road, Witness,* and elsewhere. He has been awarded several fellowships and prizes, most recently a Massachusetts Cultural Council Fellowship in fiction, and *The Literary Review's* Charles Angoff Prize. He is Writer-in-Residence at Emerson College in Boston and also teaches in the Stonecoast MFA Program at the University of Southern Maine.